'It's a rare book that gives life to ⟨...⟩ lived. *The Adversary* is stunning in its honesty, astounding in its intimacy. Warm, sexy, bittersweet, and capacious – the boy-meets-boy-meets-boys debut I've been waiting to read for a long, long while. We're simply lucky to have it.'

Bryan Washington

'By turns claustrophobic and euphoric, intimate and defamil-iarising, this slow-burn novel is smart, strange and utterly compelling. The kind of book that will have you missing the characters and wondering what they're doing long after you greedily consume its final pages.'

Emily Bitto

'*The Adversary* is moving, moody, surprising, funny and wonderfully clear-eyed storytelling. Scott is a sharply obser-vant master of the sexual and social lives of a group of friends, all in the process of becoming who they hope to be. This book doesn't just engage the reader, it captures us.'

Amy Bloom

'Sharp, clever and fizzing with the kind of anxiety that provides a brittle edge to the gorgeousness of youth, *The Adversary* is a hilarious ride through queer Melbourne. If Evelyn Waugh had lived in Melbourne and had access to Grindr maybe he would have written *The Adversary*. Luckily we have Ronnie Scott.'

Krissy Kneen

'Ronnie Scott captures the ironic cadence, casual obsessions and gay neuroses of a generation and delivers something wryly funny, very endearing and – in the best possible way – too real.'

Benjamin Law

'A story built with minute, metropolitan detail. The climax is not about overcoming so much as discovery, of oneself and others.'

Joshua Badge, *Archer*

'Further proof that Scott is an impressive writer . . . His characters are men I have known, men with whom I have lived, hooked-up, been frustrated . . . Outlanders who have ventured inwards for studies and zest . . . Scott maps a group of men who have been under-represented in popular Australian fiction.'

George Haddad, *Sydney Review of Books*

'Writing with the assurance and authority that belies his status as first-time novelist, Ronnie Scott reveals the contradictions of the human heart and the complexities of friendship, love and sexuality. Compulsively readable.'

Simon McDonald, *Written by Sime*

'Speaks eloquently of the season of youth . . . A delightful disillusionment plot.'

Vanessa Francesca, *ArtsHub*

'A triumph . . . This is a book about platonic relationships and the mysterious desires for them; it's about the kindness and curiosity it takes to search and maintain meaningful human contact.'

Peter Polites, *Reading Like an Australian Writer*

'Full of verve and humour, the characters drawn with vitality . . . You'll bask in the summery haze of *The Adversary* long after you've finished reading it.'

Dan Shaw, *Happy Mag*

PENGUIN BOOKS

THE ADVERSARY

Ronnie Scott is the author of *Salad Days*, a Penguin Special; *The Adversary*, a novel which was shortlisted for a Queensland Literary Award and the Australian Literature Society Gold Medal; and *Shirley*, another novel. He teaches Creative Writing at RMIT.

ALSO BY RONNIE SCOTT

Salad Days
Shirley

THE
ADV
ERS
ARY

RONNIE SCOTT

PENGUIN BOOKS

PENGUIN BOOKS

UK | USA | Canada | Ireland | Australia
India | New Zealand | South Africa | China

Penguin Books is part of the Penguin Random House group of companies,
whose addresses can be found at global.penguinrandomhouse.com.

Penguin
Random House
Australia

First published by Hamish Hamilton, 2020
This edition published by Penguin Books, 2023

Cover design by Laura Thomas © Penguin Random House Australia Pty Ltd.
Cover image courtesy Marcel/Stocksy.
Lines from Amy Witting's 'A Rose is a Rose . . .' courtesy
Margaret Connolly & Associates.
Typeset in Adobe Caslon by Midland Typesetters, Australia.

Printed and bound in Australia by Griffin Press, an accredited
ISO AS/NZS 14001 Environmental Management Systems printer.

A catalogue record for this
book is available from the
National Library of Australia

NATIONAL
LIBRARY
OF AUSTRALIA

ISBN 978 1 76134 341 4

This project has been assisted by the Commonwealth Government through the Australia
Council, its arts funding and advisory body, and the City of Melbourne.

penguin.com.au

MIX
Paper | Supporting
responsible forestry
FSC® C018684

We at Penguin Random House Australia acknowledge that Aboriginal and Torres Strait Islander
peoples are the Traditional Custodians and the first storytellers of the lands on which we live
and work. We honour Aboriginal and Torres Strait Islander peoples' continuous connection to
Country, waters, skies and communities. We celebrate Aboriginal and Torres Strait Islander
stories, traditions and living cultures; and we pay our respects to Elders past and present.

For Mum, Dad, Pete and Mandy

PART 1

DANCE OF THE HUMBLE MOSQUITO

Beauty that knows no love,
sorrow or pity
repeats the colours of
the burning city.

Amy Witting

A smart man once told me to be careful around gifts, as they're often more complicated than they first appear. The savviest recipients plumb their gifts for hidden questions, such as what secret agenda has been furthered by this gift? And why have I been chosen to receive it?

The smart man who said this had just given me a gift, which caused me to regard it with considerable suspicion. It was a birthday gift, and it came to me from my housemate Dan, who explained that although the gift at first may have seemed innocent – it was a month's membership to the Brunswick Baths, a gym ten minutes' walk from our crumbling townhouse – what he really wanted was to give me a reason to get out of the house, something he'd noticed happening much less through-out the winter, meaning he came home from work or his boyfriend's apartment and was not able to spend any time in the house by himself.

'But don't stress,' he finished. 'Nothing's wholly altruistic. Why do you think the gift horse doesn't want you near its mouth? That's where it keeps its money and its motives.'

I used the gym a few times that month, the deepest dark of winter, but when September came, and with it spring, I did not renew the membership; the gym contained too many fluids, too many weird-eyed men, and one day I finished a full forty-minute workout before realising I had done so while wearing a pair of jeans, a situation that filled me with a queasy kind of terror. No good things come to animals that stop paying attention to their surroundings. It suggested a particular evolutionary fate.

But I was reminded of Dan's advice just a few months later, when I happened to meet a few pretty interesting gift horses, and sometimes even had to work out what to do with their mouths – if I should kiss them, scrutinise them, grab a towel and wipe them down? I was often given gifts that summer, free advice, free rides, and in all cases these gifts were most completely understood not as magic freedoms, being hurled around the world, but always as the leavings of complicated creatures, some of whom wore costumes that concealed their intentions.

There was no hiding in our house, and Dan had not been wrong to want me outside of it at least some of the time. It was a townhouse on Park Street between Lygon Street and Sydney Road, with a half-view of the fountain at the north end of the park, the hesitant edge of dirt tracks and bike-lock-beringed light poles, the thin-grassed area that guarded its vast, green, jogging innards. Behind the sloping balcony, through two windows that clunked, were my room and Dan's room, and downstairs was the kitchen and the weedy little yard.

The house was long and narrow, with large bedrooms and loud floors, and I always had the feeling, moving up those shaky stairs, of stepping up and down the house's secret central organ, an old muscle that wasn't going to take it anymore.

It was a slow tram into Carlton, and a quick walk to Barkly Square, where I'd recently decided to shop at the tactical hours of dusk and dawn, so I had more chance of running into people from uni and engaging them in friendly conversation.

I was definitely not a shut-in. I had this thought all the time. I was just a guy standing in front of a door and almost never opening it, because I'd finished my assignments, and swot vac, and exam block, and also because my youth allowance was at its most effective in funding a life spent quietly indoors.

I thought the Barkly Square idea was clever and inspired, and it wasn't until I voiced the plan to Dan that I realised these were not the main qualities it signified.

'Making friends at dusk and dawn,' he said. 'Like the humble mosquito.'

Possibly because it was met with this response, I never enacted the mosquito plot.

I ramped up my showers as spring stretched on, I read a lot of books; I discovered a dark red at the Mediter-ranean Wholesalers that cost four dollars even but was absolutely good. I drank on the balcony in the drowsy light of dusk, which was sticking around later and later, an orange presence reaching from the eights into the nines.

Everything smelled like jasmine and looked like jacarandas. The clocks added their hours. Then one Saturday morning I woke up to a text that turned out to have substantial repercussions.

'WHAT R U DOING TONIGHT WOULD U COME OUT WITH US PLS DAN.'

Dan, who used to send amazing text messages –

'WHAT is the numerical version of the alphabet? If A is the first in the alphabet, 1 is the first in the WHAT?' – had lately become the tersest texter to have walked the earth, writing messages in a neutral form of old-fashioned chatspeak, like he was taking an early shot at being a suburban dad: 'CAN U PICK UP THE AGE,' he'd write. 'HAVING A GOOD DAY U.'

It was an interesting gesture, but difficult to support when I knew he had the full deck of syntactic possibilities at his disposal, and when catch-up opportunities were thinner on the ground than they had been this time a year ago.

He was sitting in the kitchen in his thick bathrobe of deep green, casually opening the weekend paper to the quiz page and smelling the surface of a cup of homemade brew. It was warm today already, it would hit thirty degrees, and the sweatiness of his dressing gown would somehow be the point of wearing it: a general refusal to roll with the punches, especially if no punches were right then aimed at him.

'Hi,' he said.

'You want me to come out tonight,' I said.

He peered over his paper, a wonderful prop.

'We would like you to come out tonight,' he said.

'We' was he and Lachlan, who was also in the kitchen, leaning on the bench and also drinking coffee, heavy in the matching deep green robe he called his own.

Lachlan looked at me seriously. He nodded at me seriously. He was a serious person, a serious Lachlan, a serious boyfriend for my housemate Dan. And I was not against this, at least not every part; but I could not help resisting the very swift progression from his Fitzroy apartment into our lives and home, first hooking up with Dan, then sleeping in Dan's room, then some-times appearing in the kitchen in the mornings, where he stood stoically waiting for Dan to finish shower-ing and then shepherding him out of the house and to their jobs.

The truth was that this was an increasingly rare scenario, because Dan stayed at Lachlan's more and more of the time. I probably would go out tonight because I knew that if I didn't, I would go to sleep by myself at this townhouse in Brunswick with Dan and Lachlan having gone to bed in Fitzroy, given that Lachlan's Oxford Street apartment was closer to the queer party they planned to attend.

'Who'll be there tonight anyway,' I said.

'Nobody knows,' said Dan.

I stared at him. He stared at me. This was a frequent pattern.

'You're just going out tonight with nobody else there?'

'Yes,' he said. 'As a couple.'

'Doing what?' I said.

'Drinking and talking.'

'Drinking and talking?'

'It only sounds fake when you say it back like that,' he said.

'Chris L will be there,' said Lachlan.

'Will he,' I said.

Dan closed his eyes, because the jig was up: Lachlan had exposed the ulterior motive.

Chris L was a fearsome person we used to call Mysterious Chris, both for the long silver cape he wore in his internet photos and for his large, black, bug-eyed sunglasses. Sunglasses are not mysterious in and of themselves, they are only covering two things, and both of them are eyes, but taken together, and applied consistently, a silver cape and large sunglasses in multiple pictures created a vibe that was mysterious indeed.

He was the news that walked like a man, and I did not understand how he had ended up living with Lachlan, the man who stood like a plank. But this difficult-to-process fact is exactly what I'd learned not very long after Dan had started sleeping over at Lachlan's apartment. Their living together suggested that Lachlan was more mysterious than he seemed, or that Chris L was less mysterious than we'd judged him to be. I did not know which scenario was more likely.

Recently, Dan had been treasonously suggesting that I should make an effort to meet and befriend Chris L, which was clearly not to do with our personal similarities but instead to do with making life easier for Dan, the idea being that Chris L and I could bond and create an atmosphere conducive to the construction of a wider friendship group. This way, Dan, who had once walked into my room, apropos nothing, and told me that he felt oppressed by the doctrine of queer family, could have me in place, and Chris L in place too, the better to advance his own romantic ends – a family in two houses, with Chris L and me like children, and Dan and Lachlan doubling in the role of dad.

I was not against being in place – I was proud of my stillness – but I was against, as we all are, being crudely manipulated by those who know us well enough to more finely pluck our strings. There was no finesse in this plan. Real friendship took effort. I would not give them the pleasure of participating.

'Hey, Lachlan,' I said.

He looked at me, alarmed.

'I heard Chris L lathers and rinses, but never repeats. Is that true?'

'Come out with us,' said Dan.

'Why?'

'It's important,' he said.

I rolled my eyes around the room and walked them up the stairs.

Later that afternoon, after Lachlan had left – I knew when he'd gone home from the absence of his baritone voice as much as the footsteps down the creaky stairs – I walked across the landing between my room and Dan's.

His door was ajar. This was not necessarily an invitation to chat: one of the charms and horrors of our house was that doors had to be wrenched into their doorframes, then lifted up until you heard the click of the bolt in the latch, a consequence of Brunswick being built on sinking ground.

Dan was lying on his bed and looking at his laptop. I stood there pressed up against the gap in the doorframe until he noticed me out the corner of his eye and jumped.

'Hi,' he said suspiciously.

'*Hi*,' I said.

I went in and sat on the bed. He went back to his laptop. I looked around the room at his books and plants and clothes, and the two green dressing gowns hung on hooks like dead green men. I knew so much about this room, where the bowl of silver coins was, and where he kept his antiretrovirals, and the dregs of his pouch. I knew which drawers were boring, full of irrelevant things, and which drawers might contain objects of benefit to me.

'I need one more reason to come out tonight,' I said.

He looked up from his laptop and once again peered at me, his favourite expression, curling the recipient in a cone of scrutiny.

'So think of one,' he said.

Then he went back to his weekend, his vacation from a working week I could not comprehend.

I was back in my room, lazing on the bed, when I heard his wardrobe open, and his footsteps descend, and the front door open, and the front door close.

I went and investigated. His nice new shoes, white and clean and puffy, were gone, which suggested he would not come home before going out for the evening. I went down into the courtyard and looked at his herbs. I lay on the bed and looked at the corner.

The obvious reason to go out was the onset of summer. It was November 30, the last day of spring, and summer was traditionally a time of public appearances and self-discoveries. Could I build a case against this? Not against the temperature, which was a fact of record, but against the need to humour it with summery behaviour. Like everybody, I spent twelve months of the year preparing for weather – I had no patience for the false belief that weather is dull, it was hard to think of anything more consequential – but it was disturbing to contemplate the way its implications might be used to influence behaviour. This time last year, a group of people at my uni had made fun of the Bureau of Meteorology for calling certain nights 'oppressive', this being one of the more innocuous instances of oppression and yet one of the only times the word was used by a government body. But, in a certain light, it was a reasonable judgement, given the expectation that summertime be fun.

I felt grubby after the conversation with Dan because it worked on the assumption that I was pointless and depressed, when in fact I was mostly happy and did have a point, which was to read books, take a break from study, and stare all day at Grindr, none of which are activities that harm the fabric of society. They are the same kinds of activities as having a boyfriend, having a job when appropriate, spending time at clubs – just drinking and talking – or smelling the wholesome surface of a coffee cup.

I was worried that in all this hasty talk of summer behaviour, I was not getting enough credit for the careful way I had conducted my life through the end of spring. I had recently impressed myself with a newfound ability to walk down the tender staircase and grab a cleanskin, retrieve a glass, fill it to the tippy-top, and walk it back upstairs, all in perfect darkness, all without spilling a drop.

As the day turned to its bluest hour, blue and late and sour, going out came to seem not just intolerable but impossible – not when I could be lying there with my head close to the window and listening to the washing in and out of cars on Park Street. What I mostly wanted was to hang around by myself, and I wondered what Dan would say if I told him so.

On hook-up apps I'd long since made the horrible commitment of turning myself into one of those negative-zone profiles, black squares that told you nothing interesting about themselves except that they were watching you and everybody else. When I was a teenager, in my small seaside town, I'd represented myself with a languid, ailing-looking selfie that made me uncomfortable not because the photograph was bad but because it was a true and faithful representation of the subject. This suggested it was best to conduct my business in secret, and confirmed the disappointing feeling I'd had when I came out: that I'd been swindled into giving up what might turn out to be the most interesting secret I would ever have. By becoming a black square I felt like a fixing agent, jellied and businesslike and quivering.

Because everyone appreciates a blank square that is super chill and mellow, I still seemed to scoop up as many drifts of Hi mates and What's happenings as anyone.

'heyyyy' a person said.

'heyyyy,' I wrote back, quicker to type the letters out than copy-paste the message. I went and showered. When I emerged it was night, and I was so hot from the shower I could barely peel my socks and undies on. There was no wine left in the house, just the bottles of gunk on the top shelf of the pantry from the people who'd lived in the house before us, Erins and Steves whose mail was still delivering.

When I came back upstairs, a message on my phone. 'big plans tonight? ;-P'

I sent the guy a picture, very square, very clear, nothing below the neck, like it had to pass approval by the passport scrutineers. I admired his profile, an anonymous white person in his early mid-twenties, a bit older than me. In a beer garden, at the gym, at a music festival; I swiped through the pictures, it was all the classics.

'Yeah big plans,' I said.

He wrote back straight away. 'oh yeah?'

'Yeah.'

'where?'

I blinked at the phone. I didn't want to say where, because it was here. But I guessed I was too drunk – on a glass of gunk on ice – to read a book or even pay attention to a movie, so I might as well go out and do things.

I did not trust the developers of these janky hook-up apps, which stole and leaked locations, words and pictures, so I sent him my mobile number, saying, 'Sorry, the app crashed.' But because free will is a problem that has yet to be vamoosed, he continued asking questions in the same leaky in-app chat screen, and on the screens of every government in the Five Eyes group.

His profile read, 'If it's on, it's not on ;-P', which sounded very modern, Zen and fun, kind of like saying there was no 'there' there.

'Was thinking about Fitzroy,' I typed, sighing to no one.

I walked away, but buzz, buzz. He said, 'I'm going to fitzroy'.

'Oh yeah,' I said. He had distance on; barely a kilometre. 'So give me a lift.'

'great' he said.

I stared at the phone.

I stared out the window.

'Great,' I said.

I put on a short-sleeved shirt, and also put on jeans, because this was only ten at night on November 30 and by midnight it would probably be cool-to-cold again. I explained to the stranger I was not quite ready yet and went into the bathroom and paced it in my shoes, counting my notes and coins and managing my silhouette by tucking my earbuds into the rolled cuff of my jeans. I went onto the footpath and stared down oncoming cars, the joggers' edge of Princes Park, its shadowy middle.

When the person picked me up, he was apparently post-gym, in a grey shirt with black blooms where it stuck against the skin.

'Hey,' he said.

'Hey,' I said. 'I'm just going to Fitzroy.'

'You already told me that,' he said.

'Oh yeah,' I said.

He drove down Park Street towards Nicholson, past gelati-eating couples and long rectangles of road-side space, blank with grass.

'So,' I said. 'Thanks for the lift.'

'No, it's easy,' he said.

He looked at me, smiled at me, and looked away again, being a calm and responsible driver.

We drove a while in silence, past a church, a pizza place, following the sloping road towards Alexandra Parade.

'So what were you doing in Brunswick,' I said.

'Just the gym,' he said.

'Oh cool,' I said. 'What kind of gym?'

More silence.

'What do you mean what kind of gym?' he said.

'I don't know,' I said. 'A night gym?'

He looked at me strangely.

As he did this, I noticed his hands massaging the steering wheel; the traffic was stalled at the intersection ahead, with very few cars funnelling left on Alexandra Parade. I watched another green light turn yellow and then red.

'I don't think you really want me to tell you about my gym,' he said.

'Okay, don't worry about it,' I said.

He looked at me, smiled, and looked away again. The light turned green, then changed again to yellow.

'It's a nice place,' he said. 'Not super busy. I have a routine.'

He was squeezing the steering wheel with both his hands.

Then whatever stalled us freed us and the car moved forward again. I could feel his tension easing.

'You tried to make me tell you so many boring things,' he said. 'I almost told you about my gym routine.'

'That's okay,' I said again. I was counting the cross-streets.

He looked over at me meaningfully.

'I can tell you have a really generous heart,' he said.

'Just anywhere here,' I said.

He checked his blind spot and pulled into the bike lane.

I unclicked my belt.

'Nice to meet you,' he said.

I'd already opened the door.

'What?' I said.

'Nice to meet you,' he said.

'You too,' I said.

I left the car and closed the door behind me.

The queer night had spilled into a long dark lane, which opened into a parking garage. Everyone was smoking, some people holding cans, like this was a house party and not really a bar.

They were polished, pleasant, murmuring, huddled closely in the night: Dan and Lachlan, both in shorts, sleeves pressed crisp and perfect. Dan, whose ramrod posture had met its match in Lachlan's, was regarding the people around him with one swivelling eye. Lachlan was deeply drunk and gazing liddedly at his phone.

I navigated through clumps of people and threw myself towards Dan and Lachlan. And, as I did, a small dark shape unmelted from the wall next to them.

It was Mysterious Chris, wearing a sheer black

shawl, which I guessed was more of a night look than his traditional silver cape, but because it was less theatrical it was also more strange.

I stared at him. His dark glass eyes stared back at me, for he was wearing his large sunglasses, despite the night-time hour, like a nocturnal creature with an unguessable specialty.

'This is my housemate,' said Dan and Lachlan at exactly the same time.

They looked at each other.

'Did you just say . . .?' said Dan, while Lachlan said, 'Did I just do . . .?'

They smiled at each other, excited about being so cute.

'You guys,' I said.

I rolled my eyes at Chris L.

'It's nice to meet you,' I said, and Chris L said, 'It's nice to meet you,' at exactly the same time.

'Oh —' I said.

I squinted.

His unreadable, sunglassed face.

'Did you do that on purpose?' I said.

But Chris L only watched me, then detached fully from the wall and walked past me towards the mouth of the parking garage, stalking in his shawl into a group of three tall women who closed ranks around him like choreography.

'You met Chris L,' said Lachlan.

'I think he's high,' said Dan.

'Oh,' I said again.

'Your mouth is slightly open,' said Dan.

'I know,' I said. I hadn't known.

I am not going to use this space to complain about my looks, because even though I was not the sexiest nut on the gumtree, you can do a lot with anything, actually too much, and in my case, being sickly, sort of starey and inert, did not stop me from getting rides to Fitzroy with random strangers, which was enough to make you wonder. But I knew that it was easy to invent connections when no connections are there; such is the fate of homosexual boys in every high school, who lock eyes with boys across the room and think they like them back, when all those boys are doing is sensing movement in the room and responding in accordance with their instincts.

This knowledge of what was possible, of our susceptible hearts, was what stopped me from following Chris L into the crowd – even when his face appeared through the tall group of strangers, directing its glassy circles back towards me.

It took a minute of listening to a deep, dull conversation between Lachlan and Dan, who were planning a weekend trip to country Victoria that I wasn't invited to and would not have gone to anyway, before I looked over at Chris L again and saw he was still there, still alone, possibly having just looked away.

'I'm just going to go talk to Chris L,' I said.

'Great,' said Dan.

I walked towards the strangers, and around them, and through.

'Is this okay?' I asked Chris L.

He nodded.

Chris L reached under his shawl and withdrew two bottles of screw-topped beer. The bottles had been against his body, which was not my favourite thing, but I watched him unscrew the bottles and accepted one anyway, thinking about the possibility of sweat and skin flakes.

'How did you get here?' he asked.

'That's a funny story,' I said.

I took a drink of my beer.

'And I guess I'll tell it. I found this guy online and he just gave me a lift here. And he didn't even want anything. He just, like, gave me a ride.' I took a deep breath. I smiled and kept drinking.

'Do you mean like Uber?' he said.

'What? No, I —'

'Hey.'

A guy appeared out of the group of loitering drinkers. How did *he* get here? He was nowhere, and then here.

'Hi,' said Chris L, in a deeper, more fluid voice.

The man was the same height as me, but at first I didn't know it, because he was mooching towards us, wearing a crumpled linen shirt, his hands sunk deep in khaki pockets. Despite this mooching, which I recognised instantly as the attitude of boys who were charming to mothers and otherwise up to no good, he was also a lunger, in scuffed chukka boots.

'Hey,' he said again, mooching forward, lunging further. His socks were pulled up high, whereas straight guys push them low.

'Hi,' repeated Chris L.

Chris L handed him his beer.

'Mmm, thanks,' he said.

The man was American. He took a voluptuous gulp, vocal and expert, smacking his lips all over it before handing it back to Chris L.

I thought about offering him mine, which would have been bizarre, but being around these two people as they toed closer towards each other, smiling and making sounds and saying basically anything, made me want to do something impulsive. First I would scull the beer, then I'd pour it all over my shoe. Afterwards, I'd eat the shoe, and then start licking my toes. It was just awkward to be around people who were hooking up, especially when it was awkward to be around them anyway. Chris L's mouth was moving soft and fast, so I guessed he probably was high.

'I think I should go to the bathroom,' I said.

'No, don't,' said Chris L.

The man smiled at me, this American. 'Are you sure, mate?' he said.

I liked it, wrong and queasy; the tangy Aussie word with a weird American twist. 'Uh huh,' I said. I took a step away from them.

'Come back and see us,' said Chris L.

The American smiled next to him.

'No,' I said.

'Okay,' he said.

I was a bad improv partner.

'Sayonara,' said the American.

Back at the wall where I'd left Dan and Lachlan, there was no more them. I scanned around. I saw two shorts-wearing figures walking off, away from the highway and into the quiet, house-packed streets.

'Hey,' I called.

Sayonara! Was he being insensitive or ironic? He had maybe ten years on me, maybe twelve on Chris L. Either way, it was weird and embarrassing.

'Hey!' I called again.

One of the walkers was in luminous, fat white sneakers. 'Hey!' I called. Dan.

Both of them kept on walking.

I trailed them for a long time, which was fun, and then not fun. Lots of people drove in to Fitzroy on Saturday nights and most of them thought they could find backstreet parking. When Dan and Lachlan crossed a street, I followed at some distance, frequently having to dodge the movements of these cars, which probed around like orcas, false of eye, fixed of motive.

Soon I was close enough to hear their conversation. 'What about this one?' Dan was saying.

'No, what about *this* one?' said Lachlan.

They had said it several times before I understood that they were picking houses, ones they favoured less or more, which is not something Dan and I had ever done as a drunken sport. This was slightly unnerving, so I hung back more.

'Careful, babe,' Lachlan was saying, 'there's glass up there.'

'It's fine,' said Dan, 'I'm wearing shoes,' and took a step forward, stomp, stomp, in his fancy sneakers, which caused the broken glass to snap and crunch. I laughed. It was two of my favourite Dan things, equally extreme and factual.

At the sound of my laugh, they turned around.

'Hi!' I said.

They stopped and both looked back at me.

I hugged my arms and hurried closer. When I reached them, they still didn't say anything. I heard a round of laughter from an invisible courtyard, and caught the secret smell of cigarette smoke.

'Are you going back to your place?'

They looked at each other.

'We . . . can,' said Dan.

I put my hands on my hips. Dan put his on his.

'You guys,' I said.

'We're not in a hanging-out space,' he said. 'What do you want me to do?'

'I don't want you to do anything,' I said.

'Sounds good,' he said.

'Dan,' said Lachlan.

Dan looked at Lachlan, which really let me know I was in trouble; I should not have needed Lachlan on my team.

'You tried really hard to get me to come out,' I said.

'I tried sort of hard. We were there for *hours*.'

'I was getting ready,' I said.

Dan looked at my jeans and shirt.

'Lachlan, was it really hours?' I said.

Lachlan raised his eyebrows.

'You don't have to answer that,' I said.

'It was hours,' said Lachlan.

'Oh,' I said.

It was all supremely hopeless, and Dan looked amused.

'Don't smile,' he said, even though he was the one smiling. 'We were both waiting for you. You're completely in the wrong.' He gathered himself and tried to look stern. He said, 'Thank you for coming out.' He said, 'I'm sorry we want to go.'

'Whatever,' I said. 'Where are you even going?'

'Nowhere. Somewhere personal.'

I stared at him.

He shrugged. He was over it.

'See ya,' Dan said.

'See ya,' I said.

'See ya,' said Lachlan.

I stood there in the street until they turned off and disappeared to wherever they were going.

Somewhere personal!

When I got home, it was after midnight and the spring was over.

When Dan had finished uni and started work as an assistant at an interior design firm, his induction had included an icebreaker activity wherein participants were tasked with devising three-second impersonations of their friends and families. He'd come home that night. 'Wanna see yours?' he said.

'Nope,' I'd said, but he went ahead and showed me anyway. He marched down the hallway with his shoulders thrust back, then stopped abruptly, frowned, mimed removing a pair of earbuds, sighed, and said, 'Sorry?'

It was devastating in its accuracy. Terrible in the qualities it chose to highlight, to the exclusion of others. It also had the knock-on effect of reinforcing this behaviour, which I began to think of as especially 'me'. So when I woke up in the morning, with all my disturbing questions – Where was 'somewhere personal'? Had I really met Chris L? – what I really wanted was to go out into Brunswick for a good long walk, with earbuds in and nobody bothering me.

But Dan was in the kitchen when I got up, having come back to Brunswick anyway for an exercise class, and he came through with a textbook opportunity.

'I want a second coffee,' he said.

'You got it.'

I was proud of my capacity to provide for him because I had not actually dispensed any cash last night. He nodded, and unleashed me into the world.

The sky had been uncovering inscrutable new blues and the walk to the coffee place was washed with sweet warm light. Someone on some street had put a deckchair on the corner, then a neighbouring house had added a large candelabra, a pile of bricks and an old dresser whose smudged mirror had cracked. Now the streets were filled up with free goods and easy pickings, a hard rubbish week that had crossed no councillor's desk.

I felt like a neighbourhood man, someone who might at any moment acquire plants and kids and cars. This was the exact kind of person who was liable to mouth something that caused us headphone-wearers to stop and say 'Huh?', but despite the friendly weather, we all kept to ourselves, the friendliest of all possible outcomes.

'What's Brunswick going to look like in a billion years,' I said when I got home.

'Good question,' said Dan, took the coffee from my hand, looked at me briefly, nodded, and sat back down at the kitchen table.

He looked deep into his phone; I could tell from the colours it was just a gossip site. I kept looking at him, to show him that the conversation was still going, but he was busily pretending that I wasn't in his line of sight.

'For instance,' I said, 'it might look exactly the same, or completely different. And those are just the two most extreme possibilities.'

He looked at me. I didn't say anything. He looked back at the phone.

In fairness to Dan, we had officially reserved the kitchen table as our 'reading space', not our 'conversation space', a zoning designation that had predated our move. Over the eighteen months in which we'd shared this home it had remained one of our most popular and comfortable decisions. But could it not be argued, on this particular day, that I had ventured out last night exactly on his say-so, had now brought him a coffee, and could expect a debrief? I pictured Lachlan and Chris L two suburbs over, in their unimaginable apartment, a shiny concrete void, doing whatever they did with their own Sunday mornings. Maybe the American would even skulk out of Chris L's room, his linen shirt still more attractively rumpled.

I went and showered, wetting and drying, came back downstairs, and caught Dan coming out of the kitchen.

'About last night,' I said, moving boldly towards him.

He squinted at me. 'Oh no,' he said.

'Oh yes,' I said.

He was frozen in the doorway.

'Did you have a good time?' he said.

'*No*,' I said, and leaned in. 'It was so embarrassing. You know I don't want to be friends with Chris L. *You* don't even like him.'

'So?' he said. 'We're stuck with him.'

Ugh, I thought. 'I'm not,' I said. 'And neither are you. He's not . . .' I moved my hands around in the air, summoning help. 'A law of physics.'

'You should still be nice to him.'

'Why?'

'It would make my life easier.'

'I always make your life easier.'

He raised his eyebrows. 'Like now?'

This was unfair, because we both did many things to make each other's lives easier and also obstructed each other in countless tiny ways. If we counted them up and balanced them out, the outcome would still be that the universe doesn't maintain a classical balance of cheer and woe, and everyone has to figure out for themselves how they feel about the totals.

This conversation was working me up like a chittering rodent, because we were dangerously close to the fact I did not like Lachlan, and this was both a foundational truth and completely unsayable. I did sort of like Chris L, and this too was unsayable because there was no basis for liking him, except his fashions and the briefest glimpse of his general mien. These facts seemed to hold the risk of mutual exposure, since they were both secrets about whether I liked someone or not.

Dan drummed his fingers on his lips, the habit of a boy who'd once smoked, and would still probably like to, but had finally taken the advice of his GP and now only smoked with Lachlan when they were drunk.

'Come to the pool today,' he said.

'Sure,' I said. 'Which one?'

'Fitzroy.'

'No thank you,' I said.

'Come on,' he said cheerily. 'It'll be thirty degrees.'

I knew this, clearly, as I knew all of summer's details. It was newsier than Chris L, it was newsier than news.

'Why does it have to be Fitzroy,' I said.

'Because I like it,' he said.

'Oh please,' I said. 'You're keeping secrets.'

He shrugged as if to say, sure I'm keeping secrets, I'm being secretive, you got me, making his eyes look innocent and shouldering past me.

'You're keeping *secrets*,' I yelled after him.

'And the answers you seek are in the future,' he intoned. 'At a location I have already conveniently revealed.'

I knew this would be a boring secret – let me guess, Chris L will be there – but I also knew that I would definitely go. For a person who spent a lot of his time safeguarding his freedoms, I was also an agent of Dan, a captive of his, really. I went where he wanted me, and did as he wanted, and for a long time, in this way, I was happy.

Dan once told me there are two kinds of men: the ones who get away and the ones who lose them. I found this statement almost too amazing. Not because it was overdramatic – Dan had just been dropped and say what you want about unpleasant situations, they give you carte blanche to be as dramatic as you want. It was amazing because when we'd met, in my first year of uni, he'd walked drunk into a lecture on the pre-twentieth-century novel and decided to pick a fight about this exact thing: dyads.

'So you're an Austen or you're a Brontë,' our lecturer said.

Dan had laughed unpleasantly – this ultra-severe man who had shown up for the first time at the tail end of week five, presumably after submitting our developmental assignment without having met the person who would be assessing it.

'That's funny?' said the lecturer.

'That's messed up,' Dan said. 'They're lady novelists, so of course they have to be in competition. I'm sure the Brontës weren't embarking on their literary careers just so someone could tell them they were better than Jane Austen.'

'No,' frowned the lecturer. 'I'm sure they were not, but people actually say this about other writers too. You're a Tolstoy or a Dostoevsky, for instance.'

'Oh, women and Russians. Thanks, McCarthy. They're all the same to you.'

At this time I was still living at home and commuting to uni, taking the last possible hour-long train back to Geelong Station that would still get me home, by bus, another hour away. Although my family saw me as a vague and dreamy person – this seemed to be the main reason my coming out 'made sense' – I was also prone to a particularly gross kind of grade-grubbing that meant I was both horrified and weirdly turned on by the idea of swaggering in and picking a fight with a teacher, especially over something both dangerous and petty. I judged Dan's greasy hair to be 'intense'.

But he never showed up in that lecture again. I refreshed every hook-up application in which I was then enrolled, in Brunswick, Fitzroy, Carlton, uni, on all public transport, in the hope that I would see him, somewhere, and then – what?

Instead, one day, he found me. A Tuesday afternoon, in swot vac. I was in the library, reading about Harold Holt and the Easey Street Murders when I was definitely meant to be reading about something else. 'hey', he wrote. 'looking for?' His main picture was a shirtless blur, caught like a bedroom yeti. When I sent back several photos of me with friends from school, smiling in our sheeny ways at formals and sports days, he unlocked a set of pictures that I have since tried to forget, but which were indelible in the details.

I had on my mind the losses of my several virginities, not being old enough to know it is not a cat; you can kill it nine whole times and it will still come back, it always has some dumb unfinished business. I thought it would be romantic to make out in the stacks, but this was a modern library, its metal shelves low and cold, leaving us at constant risk of discovery. He also wasn't up to being subtle. He kept kissing my arms and stroking my face, and this was exciting, but he kept stroking it, investigating the same unmoving grooves.

There is no reason it can't be fun to make out with a high person, but not when they are very high and you are very not; it is a matter of disagreeing focuses. It was also daylight, too early to be this cooked, and after a very short time, which felt very long, we realised that whatever we were trying to accomplish was not going to get us the traditional result.

I typed a message the next day. 'I've seen you before,' it said. 'Coming into the lecture. Fighting about the Brontës.'

I'd always had literary quotes on my dating profiles, my headers saying things like 'Last night I dreamed I went to Manderley again . . .' But when boys engaged with this and picked up on a reference in their messages, I scrunched my nose up, yuck, those nerds. I always wanted to be messaged by someone like Dan, whose main image had showcased his gamely flaring eyes, with header text that simply said, 'No thanks.'

I remembered the awful hair, his awful, smoke-stale tonguing, mouth twisting, lips pursing. His awful, knuckled hands.

'Do you want to try again?' I wrote.

'No bud', he messaged. 'I'm a one-time special only.'

No one is a one-time special, but it sounded great.

Dan and I did friendship in a way I never had: first an after-uni coffee, then an after-coffee beer, then some after-beer leek dumplings, then an after-dinner dance, then a split crumble of sticky drug squeezed from a squishy capsule that he pretended he didn't realise he had in his bag; then hours in a bathroom in a bar on Meyers Place with our high beams on, bold beacons casting out for more, then going home dejected in a cab we could not afford.

Home was his Westgarth sharehouse, where he rented a room from a couple who thought he was both 'too there' and 'too not'.

'So demanding,' I ventured, rocking back and forth in the yard, where he was doing a very bad job of rolling me a rollie.

He peered at me and went to take a suck of his cigarette, but it was out, and there was no way to relight its saggy middle without scattering the open pouch across the floor.

'What would you be like to live with?' he said.

'Well,' I said.

'The kitchen would be a reading space, not a conversation space,' he said.

I said I had always thought this but, as a boy who lived at home, I had little idea of what might go on inside a kitchen except grabbing things from the fridge and pouring milk over cereal or making my favourite all-terrain meal, Vegemite on toast.

Part of the problem seemed to be that his house-mates were a straight couple; he alluded to 'cultural differences'. Only later did I realise a key cultural difference may have been the inconstancy with which Dan cleaned the house.

'Isn't it interesting,' he added pleasantly, 'that before the AIDS crisis, the number one cause of death for gay people was straight people?'

I stared at him. 'Is that true?'

'Sure!' he said. 'Maybe.'

'Straight people,' I said. The cause of death was straight people: it felt so skulduggerous to suggest this, tasty and glorious and just possibly true.

'They sound terrible,' I said.

'I know,' he said. 'But have you met the gay ones?'

And this was how I learned about the problem with gay men who wanted to lift the blood-donation ban but didn't understand that this would throw poz guys under the bus; the problem with the terms of the campaign for same-sex marriage, how it had reinforced the primacy of the couple as the homonormative ideal to which all queers should aspire. The problem with guys in Prahran who caked themselves with bronzer, the problem with guys in Preston who did the same thing as a joke. So here they were, the moral wilds. They were thick and wild.

In the sixth hour of my knowing him, he told me of his status. Apparently what I said was 'Whoa.' And I will always be grateful that he also dispensed info he was absolutely not obliged to dispense, choosing to see my questions as high and silly, and to consider this a sweet position rather than a thoughtless one.

Back in my idyllic wild-less seaside community I'd barely gone as far as what you might call hooking up. But I'd still managed to be one of those disagreeable people who get on apps and ask complete strangers if they are clean and safe, as if HIV-positive guys were unsafe or dirty. I didn't have the courage to take my clothes off with a person, but I still had enough courage to stigmatise people like Dan, of whom I had previously had an almost mystic understanding: I thought of a converting agent moving through the world, turning good bodies to bad bodies, then to AIDS, then to death, and then into glowing forefathers – and these were always men – who blipped into existence whenever was convenient, to remind us of the history we'd defeated and then chucked.

I knew I had to give up something valuable and personal of my own, or I'd wake up in the morning and find Dan had disappeared, the whole night nothing but a figment.

'I don't really like touching people's bodies,' I offered.

Although I did whatever guys wanted to – for instance, I'd made out with *him* – I had a problem with mouths and had wondered if, as a child, I'd had a formative relationship with a meaningful adult who had filed teeth, bad lipstick or a mixed approach to flossing. I had looked up lots of things about this problem on the internet and mostly found classifications that did not feel right; I knew that I was basically a sexual being; I kept coming across boys I almost, almost wanted. I just knew people were gross and preferred them to keep their distance, leaving space between us, preferably also walls.

Dan leaned back and assessed me, not the first time, not the last. It was the leaning back I liked. It made you feel respected one second, acutely small and laser-scrutinised the next.

'That's a toughie,' he said. 'Let's come back to that.'

The next day, he sent me a listing for a rental house.

I moved to the city with the usual fears about what sex might do, and the usual hopes about what sex might do, and in the usual scenarios I was quickly disabused. I still did not like bodies and mouths, and I decided to blame my father and his outré number of girlfriends and wives, for letting a child spend his whole life reading novels in the corner and never making me use a straw that had been sucked by someone else. Dan blamed my personality. No one thought to blame the mouths.

My dad and current stepmum helped me move, but they did not like Dan, perhaps because he referred to them as 'the wealthy industrialists' (in our seaside town, they ran an ice-cream and juice shop). They were not much of a subject of discussion here in Brunswick, in the house that we did not end up getting from a rental agency, so impossible on student incomes that we barely tried, but inherited from someone Dan had met at Sircuit and broken up with before things could start to get not-nice.

We didn't talk very much about Dan's origins either; I knew only that his parents lived on the south side, very south, and he went over there on significant holidays, returning with embarrassment and money. It was dulls-ville, the muck of youth. It lay there, thick and sucking. It always seemed like we had lots of other things to say.

We watched random, crappy films on SBS and Kanopy about the insouciance of men and the realism of the French. We never became huggers, but we did become those people you always see on the couch at the back of the party, eyes gleaming at everyone, hands just about but not quite in each other's pockets. When he got too messed up at parties, Dan hijacked the play-lists and tried to make people dance to Cat Stevens' 'Father and Son'. When we had to be separated we made sarcastic faces, beaming unspoken thoughts into each other's minds.

We were not the same person, never once. There could be no union. He deliberately ruined dates because a guy asked 'PrEP or condoms?' (like being poz and undetectable was barely an option), or because a guy said something that casually disparaged more feminine guys.

Dan once peered at me over a glass of wine and said, 'All I want in this world is the satisfaction of knowing that we got the right to marry and then not even using it, because marriage sucks.' He had once walked out of a date because a guy called it 'our yes vote'. For Dan, the plebiscite was something 'they' had done – a complicated gift, with secret money, secret motives. 'I can think of no better fate for the institution of marriage than annihilation,' he said. He refused to acknowledge this position as extreme.

By comparison, I'd once ruined a date by saying I *would* eat a person – only if they'd died already, and only if they'd asked, but these nuances were lost in the ensuing commotion. Dan and I were quite different kinds of hard-to-be-with people, the main difference being that his positions had a point.

When I pictured Dan dating someone – and I often pictured this, because I knew that he wanted it, and I was a pessimist – I pictured him with exceptional people, maybe a hectic twink, or one of those north-side guys who are both scholarly and piggy, which somehow evens out into a fixation on the moon. Instead it was Lachlan, who was just nobody. And I'd thought I could out-nobody the best of them.

At his job in Abbotsford, Dan was exposed to all manner of ideas and pressures and vectors, none of which I seemed able to parse. The onset of Lachlan was no exception. On the day in question Dan got out late (!) and had to come home via the Woolies in Abbotsford, which made things worse, because he did not like to shop at the big two.

He was scanning his items thoroughly and the equipment jammed, and when he looked around to hail a helper, Lachlan was there too, trying to hail the exact same person. It was hell, then it was late, then he was simply coming over, and just like that, my friend had been substituted with a boyfriend, while the real Dan was drip-fed nutrients in some basement cocoon, swaddled up in bodysnatcher ooze.

The other month, I'd come down to the kitchen as per normal and heard Dan and Lachlan discussing their new business shirts, whether it mattered that you could see their nipples through them. 'I used to think about the nipple question all the time,' said Lachlan. 'But these days, I just put on my shirt and go to work.'

I just couldn't compete on the level of nipple questions. After they left, I went into Dan's room and put on one of his shirts, but if the nipples were under there, I couldn't spot them.

Before I'd let my membership to Brunswick Baths expire, a trainer had written on the whiteboard: 'Remember, summer bodies are made in winter.' It sounded like an old saw trotted out by some Scandinavian detective, waiting for the lake to thaw and divulge its many bodies, creating a grisly wealth of summer overtime.

Now though, climbing the bleachers at the Fitzroy Pool, I saw it had a troubling meaning of a different kind. While I had been imagining this Scandinavian detective, other boys had been taking the advice as it was meant, girding themselves against sagginess and scrawniness and readying their bodies to greet the sunny world.

Dan and Lachlan were already up there on the bleachers, perched on towels and gazing at me through their sunglassed eyes. Neither of their towels looked particularly beachy but instead seemed lifted from some fancy hotel, in the same thick royal green as their dressing gowns. I couldn't imagine how warm and lovely it would be to cover myself in these towels in dead of winter, nor how awful it would be to do this after exiting the water on a too-hot, windless day, sweating and chlorined and sticky with sunscreen, squinting up at the gym complex that hulked over the pool. Like many aspects of Dan's life under Lachlan, the towels seemed like souvenirs from a weird other world.

I nodded to them, saw a space on the tier below them, reasonably man-sized, and made my way towards it. To spread a beach towel on these bleachers was to perform an art. It required a keen eye for towel-shaped opportunity and no undue squeamishness for disadvantaging others. As I dropped my own scrappy blue-green-spotted towel and kicked at it to spread it, the shape beside my towel rolled over and revealed itself, inscrutable behind – you guessed it – its own pair of sunglasses, these ones dramatically large and bug-eyed.

I paused mid-crouch. 'Hey,' I said.

He paused too. 'Hey,' Chris L said.

I looked up at Dan and Lachlan. We had already said hi to each other, but I was getting into the groove. 'Hey,' I said.

'Hey,' Lachlan said.

My sunglasses were always cheap and the last ones I'd bought had broken several months ago. There was nothing left to say, and nothing left to do but take off my shoes and shirt so as to complete the sense of exposure. There were more gaps on the bleachers than it looked from below, but it was hard with noise and dense with sizzly bodies; I was lucky to have found a space at all.

Only when the American was halfway up the bleachers did I realise my terrible mistake. As if to re-introduce the idea of his Americanness, he was holding two burger shapes in Lord of the Fries wrappers, obviously having left the bleachers in order to pick them up, his towel draped off his shoulders in a pretence of modesty. He was flip-flopping up the bleachers in a pair of thongs.

I held my hands out, palms up: sorry.

'Hey, no friends in the towel game,' he said.

'This is Vivian,' said Dan.

'We've met,' said Vivian.

'Yeah,' I said, rolling over and squinting up at Dan. 'We *are* friends in the towel game.'

So his name was Vivian, which I vaguely knew was one of those names that was actually old-timey masculine, like Shirley or Evelyn, and only in the present world did it sound slightly deranged.

I was trying not to think about my view of Vivian's crotch, which was encased in smooth white trunks that somehow revealed both everything and nothing.

Dan was in one of his unimpressible moods. 'What's the towel game?' he said, when it was entirely clear what we were talking about. It was interesting how that idiom, no friends in the *x* game, was something they must have had in America too, which only made it seem particularly pointless that Dan was pretending not to know what it meant.

'It's this,' I said, and said, 'Chris L, would you mind moving your towel?'

Chris L swooped his lenses over the bleachers, over the day. 'I don't mind at all,' he said.

I smiled at Dan. 'Thank you, Chris L,' and when he'd done so I moved my towel, which made it kind of bunchy, but the towel and I were both still dry, so bunchiness was fine. 'There,' I said, and Vivian set his own towel down next to me, stretched it out as far as possible, and sat down where he could.

I was very impressed with Vivian and Chris L for going along with me, although I was unsure what I had been trying to demonstrate.

'And that's the towel game,' I said, and refolded my legs.

Vivian passed a burger to Chris L over my body, causing just a drop of mayo to fall beside my chest.

We teetered on a verge made up of chlorine and the sun, now revved up, now satiated, now tired, now flushed. We were parched and oily. We were sun-drunk.

I was very happy to have found my new friends, but I wondered if I liked them mainly because they were not really talking and because all I had to do in order to be their friend was sit between them and also not talk.

'So,' said Vivian. 'How do you know Chris L?'

Chris L looped into a little pretzel of social watchfulness, unknowable behind the bright-black surface of his shades but projecting a freaky total awareness.

'We're friends,' said Chris L simply.

I widened my eyes in complete surprise; then narrowed them in calculation. Maybe Chris L was trying to establish that he was available to Vivian, and unencumbered by me. Maybe he was just being a friendly easy guy. I needed a kind of middle state, attentive and normal. I tried to relax my eyes a little and nodded with Chris L.

'What are you doing with your *face*,' laughed Dan.

Chris L whipped his neck dramatically towards him. 'Vivian's from New York,' he said, as if Dan hadn't spoken.

'Well, I live in New York,' said Vivian.

Of course. So this was interesting. And it explained something, whatever there was to explain about Vivian, which was not a lot. He wasn't an American in Australia, saying 'mate' to be sexy and fun. He was an Australian in America and coming home for Christmas, saying 'mate' for the reasonable reason that he'd been saying it his whole life. Well, he lived in New York. He probably lived in Brooklyn, one of those Australian guys who come home when their visas expire and their cash runs out. They were reliable fixtures of this pool in summer months, which gave them the air of the animal and dumb, mindlessly moving in the direction of the sun.

'Cool,' I nodded.

'New York's so,' said Vivian.

'I know,' said Chris L. 'And Melbourne's so.'

I died inside and curled over into a toothpaste worm, covering my ears as totally as possible without looking obvious and rude. I had always thought my ideal boyfriend would live in a hard-to-reach location, on a voyage or in a jail. Imagine having a boyfriend who lived in New York always, a hard-to-reach location if there ever was one. A place of close streets, pink buildings, good things and bad, don't smoke on the fire escape, pick up after your dog. It seemed tragic and interesting, to fly over the world with no sense of responsibility for where you might end up. The idea was powerful and stupid.

Was this what a crush felt like – brainless and harsh? It felt right and wrong at the same time, which meant it had to be wrong. I couldn't like Vivian, we had barely said six words. I just hadn't slept with someone in a very long time, and wet cement and chlorine had a provoking quality.

I had to do something before I did something more drastic, like find a strange excuse to lean over and touch his leg.

'Chris L,' I said, interrupting him mid-sentence. He had been saying something about guys here, or guys there, but when I held out my hand, he tilted his head towards it. He took it decisively. His mouth went very firm. It was the first time in a long time that I had held someone's hand, and I was surprised at its dryness and its toughness.

'Where are we going?' he asked me.

'Somewhere personal,' I said.

We walked down the bleachers. 'That was kind of boring,' Chris L whispered. 'Thanks for saving me.'

The day was hot, the walk was short, then we were at the water. 'No problem,' I said.

He jumped into the pool.

He came up for air laughing and saying something else. But I was already walking back up the bleachers, looking up at Vivian, who was looking at me.

You sometimes heard stories about things happening to guys, of walking into certain houses in certain suburbs and finding more people in there than you had expected, or opening the door one day to let a stranger in and finding you had been visited by a different stranger, a stranger you had not agreed to accommodate.

But these stories were consequenceless if you took precautions; they were in the category of repealable things, not like what happened to other people – terrifying things – and as such, our precautions were almost supernaturally useless. Dan and I left index cards at the feet of our beds on which we wrote down addresses, intended destinations. If we came home safely, we disposed of the cards, and no one would have to know we'd even left the house. If we didn't come home . . . it was unclear what then, given we'd already have met our unchangeable ends.

I loved Brunswick, the long low-ceilinged gloom of Barkly Square, the narrowness and busyness and length of Sydney Road, and further things that were personal and not based in measurement. But how difficult it was to get anywhere from Brunswick; you had to own a car, like Lachlan, or a bike, like also Lachlan, or have a job and take Ubers and sometimes cabs (like Dan), or you had to date Lachlan or Dan.

How far would Dan realistically go, if he found one of my index cards and was meant to seek revenge? Of course to Parkville, Coburg. But Richmond? Even there? It was just one suburb over from his workplace in Abbotsford, but I knew how exhausted he could get after work, and vengeance was famously all-consuming.

This was a live issue on this bright December day, because I had decided to hook up with the person who had given me a ride to Fitzroy on the last night of November, and he lived in Richmond, beyond the jurisdiction of the index cards. It was eight days after the pool, and in that time I'd been thinking increasingly sexy thoughts about Vivian. This made me want to rid myself of Vivian in the traditional fashion, but because it was a Monday morning the only people online were other students (yuck!) or guys who had gone out on Friday night and were still awake, using little icons of crystals and clouds to identify themselves.

My car-driving friend explained that he'd taken this Monday off work, at a call centre, and wondered if I'd like to come over and hang out. I saw right through this ingenious sex code. It was bright and cloudy, which put me in an adventurous mood, but no mood is adventurous enough to go from Brunswick to Richmond on the necessary mixture of buses, trains and trams.

The problem was solved by Lachlan, through no knowledge of his own, because he and Dan had driven inland to a music festival and taken off the Monday to give themselves a long weekend. They had driven to this festival from our place on Friday afternoon and left Lachlan's gorgeous bicycle tucked under our stairs.

It was a chromium monster, with hot tyres and real heft. When the stranger said Richmond, he did not mean the Abbotsford edge – this was just before the river, where the land begins to crest. I heaved the bike up the hill. My pits were soaked with sweat.

My new friend in Richmond was living in a silvery apartment block that was chunked with rainbow boxes, modern, cheap and fun, but right across the road was a yellow-brick apartment building with a messy leafy garden, fewer units, wide windows.

The stranger lived alone, which was a dream of mine, and his own stark tinted window faced the busy road, leaving the bed to occupy a zone of his studio that was windowless and permanently dark. We lay down with our clothes on and I knew that I'd messed up. We didn't really know how to touch each other properly; we lay on our sides, propped up on one arm, sort of lazily batting each other's chests and stomachs.

He tried to kiss me and I moved my lips dryly over his, on again and off again, on again and off again.

'Mmm,' he said. 'This is nice.'

He went to the bathroom for what seemed like a long time and came out with wet prints on both sides of his shirt. The grotto of his bedroom had begun to feel oppressive, taking on the smells of sex where there had been none.

A car horned outside, where it was a beautiful day, and I could smell the dry air rising off the bitumen, breezing in on shining currents, chemical and hot.

'Come and smoke with me,' he said. 'I don't do it very much.' He grinned, and did that thing where he looked at me and looked away again. Either he had once been told this was adorable and deliberately adopted it, or he did not realise he was being adorable. I was inclined to like it because it got me off the bed and out of a situation that I knew was going to get more depressing the longer we continued.

We were clothed but I still felt bare and unprotected, because the window faced the road. There were
no people down there, only rushing cars, and across
the road the yellow bricks of that art deco apartment
building, looking both eaten and rotten. In New
York you could smoke out of your window all day if
you wanted and nobody would ever have to know.
I wondered what it would be like to have that naked
anonymity, knowing you were only one of many.

'I would ask you how you went in Fitzroy last week,'
he said, 'but I can tell you don't really like questions.'

I stared at him. What a thing to say. I felt like
saying, guess what? I love questions. Guess what
I don't like, leading statements that literally beg to be
argued with.

'Where are you going?' he said.

I was going towards the door.

I spun around and pointed. 'I thought you thought
I didn't like questions,' I said.

'Wow,' he said and smiled and laughed. 'Good
one,' he said.

I instantly felt rude. This was what I got from only
spending time with Dan, who had done this exact thing
more than once, spun around and pointed in order to
'catch' me, a habit that I understood was invasive and
alarming but characterised as swashbuckling and bold.

'Maybe I'll see you around,' I said.

'Wow,' he said again.

I shook his hand.

He smiled.

I'd leaned Lachlan's bike against a light post near the
art deco apartments, on the struggling nature strip
across the busy road. When I bent down to retrieve
the helmet, I heard a voice yelling 'Mate! Hey, mate!'
from somewhere up above.

I looked up, but back over the road, in my new
friend's apartment, the many square windows were
reflective and closed. I turned and there he was,
the source of the shouting. Two hands gripped the
bricked sill of the art deco apartment, the face hidden
by darkness up on the second floor. The sun was
high and bright, and long white gauzy curtains
were billowing on either side of the figure out of the
wide window.

'Hello?' I called up.

He said nothing back.

Even though the figure was obscured by the glare,
I somehow knew from his posture and other absorbed
details that it belonged to Vivian, the man from
Fitzroy Pool. I had the skin-crawling feeling of this
not making sense, before my brain did the correcting
work of normalisation that accompanies and smooths

over coincidence. How could Vivian live across the road from my new friend, the stranger? But in a way, of course he did, because Melbourne was sometimes small, and of course I would leave the house for the first time all year and instantly run into basically the only other person I knew. It was a busy road, bordered by a million apartments. It would be evidence that we lived in a simulated world if it did *not* contain coincidences like this one.

I looked across the road to check that my other friend was not back at his window, smoking away, but the sun shone so brightly off the phalanx of windows that anyone could have been watching and I would never know. At least none of them seemed like they were open.

'Am I meant to go up there?' I asked.

But I was asking nobody; Vivian was gone.

Even though this was very apparitional and alluring, it also wasn't actually very helpful at all. I stood there for a long time, examining the brickwork and flexing my shoulders, waiting for further instructions. When none came, I walked the bike over and tried the glass door, which was unlatched, potentially forever, because I hadn't heard the click of somebody buzzing me up.

I left the bike under the stairs and climbed them. It was not a large building and I could guess the location of Vivian's apartment door.

'Hello?' I called into the door. No answer behind it.

I wondered if I should knock, but you did not need experience to understand the nature of this simple game.

I pushed the door open.

'Hi,' he rasped.

Vivian lounged in the far corner in a pair of sweatpants, with his feet kicked up on a coffee table, his back sunk in a couch's crevices. Just to add more skeeze, he was looking at his phone. The room belied the awesome brightness of the world outside; the curtains had stopped billowing and hung sheet-like out the window, gaining their own grubbiness by settling against the grimy outside wall. Between them was a slit of sky, and just the candy edge of my friend's apartment block, one of the blue cartoon chunks that topped the silver building.

'Let me start again,' he rasped. He cleared his throat. 'Hi,' he said.

I blinked at him. 'Are you sick?' He shook his head. Just skeezy.

I bobbed around the room, scrutinising.

'Ooh, bookshelves.'

All he had was romance novels, beach reads and

Lonely Planets, a couple of years out of date and stuffed with takeaway menus.

'They're not mine,' said Vivian.

Of course they aren't, I thought, with the lubricating feeling of several keys sliding into several locks at once. I wondered, but knew not to ask, because why be a dickhead, if this apartment happened to be free just whenever he wanted or only whenever he ran out of money in New York. However, this was very bitter, and besides, my own rent was humiliatingly subsidised; Dan paid fifty dollars a week more than me for a bedroom that had barely a square metre on mine, another complicated gift he had bestowed on me, and this before he'd graduated and started working full time.

It was getting up my nostrils, the darkness of the unit, the suggestion of hypocrisy, the whole greasy shebang. There was something in the layout that made the air feel stale, as if the billowing curtains had been a hallucination, the phenomenon localised and spooky. It was weird how both these men had personalised grottos, teenage-boy aesthetics played out on the scale of a single-occupancy apartment. I wondered what I would do if I ever lived alone, but could picture only our house when nobody was home.

'What's so interesting on your phone?' I said.

He held up the screen and waved it.

'Come over and see,' he said.

My legs tensed up. I said, 'Light it up and show me.'

He laughed across the void.

'Why won't you come over?'

'I don't like questions,' I deadpanned, even though this conversation had been with someone else. But actually I was very unsettled. It was weird how one person could attribute to me a sense of unquestionability but Vivian was totally unable to see the same thing. It suggested, uncomfortably, that I did not possess it, and that with Vivian I would have to rely on some other quality.

'Are you seeing Chris L?' I said.

'Not really,' he said.

That cinched it. *My* question had been clear and plain. Even though I was fun enough to come to this apartment, I was not fun enough to swim around in a quantum stew with a co-swimmer whose stakes were in another hemisphere. I wasn't friends with Chris L, was I? 'Not really' also. But I hated guys who were masc and cool, chill and casual. I had learned this from Dan, this peering-in-the-mouths-of-gift-horses, this following-the-money. A grey area could hide a lot of black and white ideas.

'See ya,' I said, and walked back towards the door.

'Hey,' he said. 'Not so fast.'

I stopped. He did not get up.

'What's your number?' he said.

I rolled my eyes and said.

'Thanks,' he said, thumbing it into his phone. 'I'm into it. You're cute.'

I seized in place.

'I'm what,' I said.

Full quiet. He said, 'Cute?'

I wanted to spit on the floor. Instead I ran downstairs, retrieved the bike, did not look at the windows; but as I'd left the room, his voice had come chasing behind me: 'You make me want to explore my sexuality,' he'd said.

I rode and rode and rode the bike. I had to get back to Brunswick.

I did not look back.

Literally all I'd done was something other than what he expected, and was there a universe in which this was resolved by Vivian re-evaluating the prevailing conditions? No, I was cute; something liked but not admired. And I made him want to explore his sexuality, which was bad for several reasons, and all of them were worse. No one in their right mind wants to explore their sexuality, all you're going to do is run into something mangy, better left untreated and unfed. It was a crazy thing to tell someone, dangerous even, so unbelievable as to be genuinely egregious.

I rode suicidally, which is hard to do on Canning Street, with its wide lanes and nature strips and student picnickers and considerate drivers and strong civic ideals, a perfect place to close your eyes and ride.

When I got home, I was met with the familiar sounds of Dan in the kitchen, busy with the preparation of some post-festival meal, and so I snuck the bike silently back under the stairs. This was easy, for Lachlan kept his bike, and all things, serviced to a noiseless state of unsqueaking zoom.

'I just flew here from Richmond,' I said, 'and boy are my arms tired.'

In making this stupid joke, I had given the game away, because no way would Dan believe I'd caught public transport to Richmond and he also knew what my bank balance looked like. But Dan's focus was elsewhere. He was bent over the sink, his hair limp and stark, and his hand was down his throat, pulling up oozy wet ropes.

'Dan,' I said, laughing, and moved towards the sink.

He held a hand up, but I kept coming. He did one of those vomity wipes that succeeds only in drawing extra, sticky vomit from further down the throat, creating a wide, solid-seeming web of spew between the fingers. He cleaned it off, but some ropes hung there stubbornly.

'Good festival?' I asked him.

'Allegedly.'

His eyes were spidered red. While I had been riding through Richmond, failing to compromise various principles that I could not defend, Dan had been driving home from the music festival with Lachlan's friends, a healthy group of professionals-in-training, two of whom had decided to spring a wedding on everyone, first luring them to a roadside stop that seemed green and normal, but quickly turned out to be filled with relatives and cake.

The speeches were about growing up, girls becoming women, boys attaining their hopeless but basically lovable place as men. A joke was made by an uncle that depended on a sense that his niece, the bride, was silly, and ought to be reined in. The men stood by in grim assent. Dan had said that he could probably have enjoyed it with a bit of warning, and Lachlan told him, 'Nobody has to be warned about a wedding.'

'I am *so* sorry he said that,' I said, though actually it was funny.

'I'm sorry too,' he blubbered, and held out his gooey hands.

'No, Dan,' I said. He stepped forward, his hands coming towards me. 'You're such a strong person. You know what always makes me feel better?'

'A hug.'

'A shower.'

When he came out of the shower, and was safely in his jamies, I made sure I was waiting right outside the bathroom door, feeling guilty for not having touched his hands before. I held out my arms in a supplicating position.

'Ugh,' he said, 'the moment has passed.'

I let him push by me in the hall, but he stopped right beside me, smelling like some new bath gel, acrid and fruity. 'Did you feed my plants while I was gone?' he asked.

The accepted term was watering. 'Yes, Dan,' I lied, because what plant cannot live three days without its meal? Weren't plant-loving people meant to be meditative and moderate? He had only wished to confuse and inconvenience me by asking in the first place, and now he sought a reason to reprimand me for something.

'It's not a huge drama if you didn't,' he said.

'No, it was good practice,' I said – staring him down, willing him to challenge me. 'I've been thinking about getting into the plant space.'

He raised his eyebrows. 'Cool,' he said. 'What did you even do today? Should we get out of the hallway?'

And I 'didn't like questions'. Ha! I liked questions so much that the only thing I liked more was getting two at once, because then I could avoid having to tell Dan a weird story about what I'd done with my day, a memory that already felt scummy. In the past, he would definitely have loved this stupid story and said 'what were you doing going to Richmond, you freak'; but the exact thing that made the story interesting, Vivian, was also what made it compromising, and best kept to myself.

Late that night, when I was cleaning my teeth, a text from an unknown number: 'hey'.

I froze. I had felt safe in the temperate latitudes of home, with Dan in his bedroom, watching *Australian Survivor* on catch-up, and me here in the bathroom, having failed to work out where he'd hidden that special new body wash and instead using the dull dregs of a classic bar of soap.

'nice to see you today' the messenger added.

It wasn't that nice to see me, I was not the Pope. But it was *very* nice to receive a message from Vivian, even if he was being as vague as it seemed he was.

I flossed my teeth and replied as thoughtlessly as possible, because there is no substitute for the true tossed-off response.

'Sure it was nice,' I wrote.

'im dying to see you' he said.

This response came almost instantly. I swallowed the floss. Not really. But we're obviously just hair and blood, pulsing through the jungle, and you never know when someone will text you on your jungle phone.

'I am sure you're not dying,' I typed.

'yes' he typed, a little gnomically, because: yes he's being dramatic or yes he's almost dead?

I decided to proceed as though the message had made sense.

'If you're SO dying to see me, why don't you come over right now?'

But I deleted 'come over right now' and replaced it with 'come for a drink', because I have lots of self-respect and also Dan was home. If luck held out, he'd be at Lachlan's by the time the drink was over, even though in all probability that just meant I would come home alone and there would be nobody to bitch to, but such are the risks of the adventurous life.

It was so misguided to meet him for a drink. But consider the alternatives. I could go to bed and text him. I could chat to someone else. Going for the drink, I could at least gain information and have another chance to consider what I'd refused. It was getting close to danger without truly courting same, a bit like I was licking just the very tip of the toad.

———

I liked the Retreat because it was close to home without being so close as to be completely obvious and sleazy; but also because the beer garden had several banks of tables with a nice view of the door, and you could see whoever was approaching before they saw you.

It was late on a Monday night and there was no one out, a couple of people inside but, out here, just no one, and I remember this because there was no one to see my face fall when the consequence of my carelessness was revealed in full.

The man who swung the door open and approached was not Vivian; it was, of course, the stranger who lived across the road from Vivian, whom I had also seen today and who, in retrospect, seemed a bit more likely to believe me 'nice to see', and to whom I had also exposed my mobile number, but who had not previously chosen to text message me.

'Hi!' he said. 'I love this bar.'

I glared. 'You live in Richmond.'

'So?' he said. He waved his keys. 'They're car keys,' he said. 'They get you where you want to go. Is this your first time with cars?'

It was all so wrong, his nice mood, his dorky joke, when in fact he represented the ruin of my plans, which I had not felt really fine about enacting in the first place, which meant they would have had to work effectively, elegantly, in order for me to think I might have done the right thing.

He once again wore a grey shirt with blooms of blackish sweat, proof he'd ended the day at his gym in Brunswick.

My heart sank, buoyed, sank. It went through squeezing ceremonies. My Richmond friend had no idea that he was the wrong man and had come to the Retreat with an honest intention.

He was looking at me searchingly.

'I need a drink,' I said.

'Roger,' he said, and disappeared into the bar.

Even this was depressing; he was too compliant! Hadn't people heard of being perfect, like Dan? I opened my phone and started writing a message to Dan, but realised that it would arrive completely context-free. It was also a further example of a missive where the energy I expended would not be sent back to me. What was he going to write? 'GREAT STORY. BYE'?

A friendship, a collection of facts, and its practice, a collection of principles.

'I love this bar,' the stranger was repeating. I'd stopped paying attention, as always, a terrible sign.

He'd returned from the bar, two gold pints in his hands; I was staring at an open, empty message screen, which hung there vulnerable and open in my hand.

'So you said,' I told him. 'Because it's near your gym?'

'Yes,' he nodded seriously. 'Because it's near my gym.'

I nodded at nothing and accepted the pint glass. He sat down.

'Cheers!' he said. He took a big gulp, and said, 'So what do you do with yourself?'

I looked at my beer. Dan had once come home from a dinner party in a rage because the host had banned the guests from saying anything about their jobs. Dan *liked* talking about his job, an assistant role that he hoped to 'parlay' into design but also enjoyed for its own labours. But I'd have rather died than tell someone I was a student, especially someone who lived alone and had a car.

I looked around for signs of a believable profession. The best I could come up with was 'I'm a beer garden salesman', but just as I was thinking about saying this, the phone that had been lit up in my hand went dark, and both our eyes were drawn to it. 'Who were you texting? Dan?' he asked.

He clapped a hand over his mouth, but he was smiling under it. I stared at him. Oh my god, I thought. Whatever this was, it was messed up.

'What's going on,' I said, in full cucumber coolness.

'Sorry, sorry,' he said. I could see his face drop. He'd meant it as a fun reveal, not a strange revelation.

I drank and drank the beer. He said, 'I truly didn't realise. Not till I picked you up.' He was blathering. He meant the weekend before, in his car. 'But I always used to see you guys hanging around at uni. You were always talking to him at the back of class.'

I could feel my eyes widen, widen. I didn't know what to do with my mouth. But then I snorted, because it was true. Dan and I had always been in the back of classrooms, giggling and gossiping and not doing our work.

'We were terrrrrible,' I said.

'No, you guys were really cute.'

The word was redeemed. 'We were super cute,' I said, and pictured Dan's chin, which he was always saying he planned to someday 'remove in full' and replace with a more creditable jawline. Dan was all I thought about, I realised again and again. I was doomed.

'What's he up to these days?'

How dare you, I thought.

'You don't live together?' he asked, winking.

I was being played with, and I tried to bring myself around to a headspace in which I could possibly enjoy this. Someone must enjoy this, or why would people do it?

'It's great, actually,' he was saying. 'I love it when guys have friends.' He shrugged. 'It just means you know how to maintain a close relationship. How many people our age can say that?'

He looked up from the pint glass, peeking for clues, assessing. He'd said this to himself in the car on the way over, it was a rehearsed speech, I was sure of it. He was proud of his open-mindedness. He had talked himself into it. It's taught me how to maintain a relationship, I thought. Sure it has. I pictured myself hanging out in my new friend's apartment, slipping out a vial of Dan's nuptial vomit that I could press against my nose whenever I felt the tug of home.

The stranger must have graduated in the same year as Dan, which made me see the universe in a whole new way. I doubted he could have lived alone while he was still at uni, and the implications chilled my bones: how quickly things could move.

'I have to confess something,' I said. It suddenly seemed very important to touch someone tonight, even someone I'd already touched today and knew I didn't like. 'I chose this bar because it's very close to my house.'

'Uh uh,' he said, wagging his finger. 'This isn't a hook-up.' He leaned over the table. 'It's better to have something to look forward to.' He winked again.

Of course that would be better, but did it seem like we would? I watched the possibilities fly like currency out of my hands.

'Well, stranger,' I said, and hesitated. I could not think of the right way to explain my reasoning without it sounding horrifying, which I guess it was. He looked at me expectantly. 'Okay, my friend,' I finished.

I held out my hand. He laughed and shook it, exactly like the handshake we'd had earlier. 'Pleasure to meet you,' he said. I smiled, because it worked so well; it was our little game.

I saluted him and marched home to the hot beat of this midnight, chance encounters, beer encounters, past a Monday bedtime, a summery encounter that could probably have been worse.

I thought of his strangely shaped arms, for all arms are strange, and the neck that moved so formlessly into his chesty front.

'goodnight :-P' he texted.

I did not respond.

The last week before Christmas took place in some future world, where everything that mattered had been hurled into tomorrow and the now was an impediment to accessing this fortune. It was a week in which the smallest things – the news, the web, the food – conspired to stall the natural action of the world, and no attempt to eat at noon, pour wine at three or four, or brush my teeth at bedtime could restore its normal motion.

There was no reason to feel like this! I'd finished classes in November and they would not resume till March, so the Christmas–New-Year's–public-holiday complex should not have held any particular sway.

But summer does sort of take you over. I showered that week because I was bored, I showered because I was sticky. We didn't have a couch, just a table in the kitchen, so I dragged my mattress downstairs and started sleeping in the lounge, in front of the open courtyard door.

I occasionally responded to text messages from the stranger, saying hey, how are you, where are you, what exactly is the plan, all of which I appreciated, this getting in my way, building a relationship through accretion of contact. 'Can't today stud!' I wrote. 'Busy, busy, busy!' I didn't know which was more horrific: another me living in a many-worlds scenario, spookily compelled to actually do all this business, or the real me, who called strangers studs, who used this kind of language.

It was also kind of great that Vivian had asked for my number and used it to do literally nothing. It was fine? There were so many things that mattered in my life that I didn't think about until I absolutely had to, my Richmond friend being just one recent example, another being a sense of pride and my strength of character, which the lack of texts from Vivian made me instantly trash. Maybe this was the real solution to the Fermi paradox. Why, when there should be many other civilisations up there in outer space, do we here on our little earth seem to be so alone? Maybe it was just that other civilisations were boring, and Vivian-like societies knew we weren't worth their time.

I had a giant, multi-day, battery-busting phone spree that was aimed at finding Vivian on any social media, including once-popular but now-mothballed photo sharing websites and pre-smartphone hook-up sites that didn't work unless you enabled pop-ups. There are more things on heaven and earth, there are other apps than these, and in none of them did there exist the phenomenon known as Vivian, a collection of animals, vegetables, minerals and mysteries.

I liked him, I realised. And it was a full-on thing. Meaning it was an ambivalent thing, because ambivalence was realistic; the doubting only made it more delicious and complex, the same way that Vegemite had to be spread very thin or you realised it was salty and unreasonable.

Maaaate. I liked him because Chris L had hooked up with him, and because he had quickly, lazily and in the end disposably demonstrated a tiny bit of interest in yours truly. Maybe these were my kinks, finally my kinks: things that belonged to other people and were indifferent to me. I thought of his smile as sphinxlike, but the truth was his smile was hardly secretive, just pretty. Still, it was sphinxlike, I insisted to myself. It was sandy and rugged. It was windswept and revered.

I wouldn't be the first person who chucked

themselves against the probability wall not because they necessarily wanted to go through it, but because they liked the feeling of their skin hitting the bricks. Why couldn't I like a pet rock, or a plant with the wings of a vulture? Why couldn't I like one of those seemingly single-minded slimes that's actually trillions of independent creatures, sludging and devouring in superficial concert? It didn't matter. I didn't like them; I liked this.

I almost called Dan one night when I knew he was at Lachlan's to tell him the good news – finding my kink, my truth – but stopped when I realised that Vivian might be over there, again proving that he was a bad idea.

This part was so unnerving that when Dan came home from his parents' on Christmas night, laden with grain salads and melty chocolate mints, he found me curled up on my mattress in front of the courtyard door, staring at a blank phone screen.

'Dan,' I said, 'am I real?'

'Yes,' he said. 'Meanwhile, have you seen what's happening on the street?'

I turned over. 'What?' I said.

'Go out and see,' he said.

'Okay,' I said, and climbed off the mattress, padded down the hallway and opened the front door to the silent Christmas street. 'Dan,' I called, 'there's nothing on the street.'

'And it's still so much more interesting than whatever's happening here. Get up, have a shower, come downstairs and eat. I really can't believe I have to say this.'

I'd already had way more than my quota of showers, but I had another one, and dried myself thoroughly on the bath sheet I'd had the foresight to hang on the balcony so it dried all stiff and scratchy in the summer wind. Was it believable that an honest person could spend this much time under water? I could build a case for it. You worked out how to live – these recreational showers – and hurled your capital into it, and against, too, such forces as would have you removed from these showers, clothed and out of doors.

But when I came downstairs, that was almost where Dan was – halfway out the door, with the bowl of parent salad in his hands.

'Hey,' I said. 'You just got home.'

'I know I did,' he said. He looked at me expectantly. 'Come on, I'm hungry.'

I put my shoes on, too pleased that we were going on an excursion to point out that it was probably not the best use of his time to stand in an open doorway, waiting for a person who did not know you were waiting, to head out on an excursion they did not know would take place.

We walked into the park and found a quiet possie by the fountain, on a sweet spot between open lawns where anyone could see us and the full dark ranges of vertiginous trees.

'I'm on holidays,' he said.

'Oh yeah!' I said. 'Happy holidays, Dan.'

He had worked right up to Christmas Eve, this was the way of the workplace.

'Thank you,' he said. 'Thank you!' He smiled. 'What's been happening?'

I could not describe this nothing week, that would be disastrous, so I took a deep breath and delivered an old rerun that would not seem like a rerun to him. I told him about my Richmond friend, starting with the part about how in the car that first night he'd kept doing that thing where he looked over at me and looked away again. 'I can picture it,' he said. 'Classic driver behaviour. What's his name?'

'Um,' I said.

I showed him my phone, where I had saved the stranger's number as 'Richmond Man'. Dan told me that I couldn't save the stranger's name like that, because if you web-searched for 'Richmond Man' you'd just find details of various bloody deaths, the kind that left you identifiable solely by your location and gender. I had thought of it more like Mitochondrial Eve or the Encino Man, two creatures known for their dignified anonymity, but we did a search for Richmond Man and the problem was real.

'But anyway,' he said, 'you like Vivian, so who cares?'

My mouth dropped open.

'It's not true!' I said.

'I knew it,' he said. 'I knew it that day at the pool. *Yes*,' he said, to underscore it. It was all so unnecessary. Why could he not reveal it nicely, this enjoyable intimate knowledge, as opposed to glowing in mean-spirited triumph?

I rolled my eyes and explained my various feelings, none of which sounded very strong or reasonable when vocalised to Dan, and described the strange event at Vivian's apartment so as to better support these feelings.

'Okay, that is interesting,' he said.

'Very interesting,' I said. 'Hey, when you've been at Lachlan and Chris L's place in the last few weeks, has Vivian, like . . . been there?'

He didn't even blink. 'Absolutely, yes,' he said.

'Oh,' I said.

He winced for me. 'But maybe they're just friendsssss?'

'Definitely. It's *so* fine, it's really not my problem.'

'Because he hasn't messaged you and you might never see him again?'

'Oh, I guess,' I said. 'I meant – nothing.'

'Okay.'

'No, tease it out of me.'

He did the opposite, focusing on the salad. He hadn't remembered cutlery, and was covering it up by claiming that it was a 'hand salad'; we picked at sticky gherkins and potatoes.

'I mean I could almost say the same about Chris L,' I said. 'I've only met him twice or something. I should do what I want.'

'True,' he said. Two strangers jogged past, a demonstration of social innocence, a model by which two people could pass by two others and everyone could choose their preferred level of involvement. 'Wait, how is it not your problem if the world's just a place where everyone does whatever they want, whenever they want to?'

'No, Dan, enable me.'

'I am,' he said. 'I'm enabling you to do whatever you like, but in full knowledge of your actions. Imagine if you stumbled into doing something tragic and I didn't help you know exactly what it is.'

More silence, no strangers.

'It would be *tragic* if I fucked Vivian?' I said.

I liked and loathed that, in this broken windows theory of dating, I was somehow responsible for our general moral health, determining what society permitted and what not.

'I guess it would depend on how you did it,' he said.

I was also troubled that Dan's best advice aligned suspiciously with his horrible plan to spark friendship between me and Chris L, which I was hoping he'd just forgotten about. How long did a plan have to be inactive before you could consider it 'not at all a plan'? I wondered how long before the Richmond Man would stop texting me, and whether the vaguely implied plans suggested by my rendezvous with Vivian had any distinction or value.

And what about the other plan, the shaky plan of me, to send me out into the world in search of love and friendship? Was there another life out there where people could just 'be' without being influenced by the plans of other people, without being positioned as participants in their schemes? I guessed this was what was called conspiracy thinking. But living with Dan meant being involved, unmistakably, at least in certain domestic-grade conspiracies. I was sure that whatever they were doing, Chris L and Vivian had not so much as the slightest 'plan' for each other, not either of them. Their summer would be purposeless, relaxing.

'Should've thought carefully before you encouraged me to go out into the world,' I said. 'Never know who I might bring home!'

'You haven't brought anyone home.'

'Oh yeah,' I said. 'But if I *did*, we could go on double dates with Lachlan and Vivian. That wouldn't be so bad.'

'I guess we'll never know.'

He put his head on my shoulder.

'Merry Christmas,' he said.

Later that night, he caught a cab to Lachlan's.

This all suggested a universe of hazy chance and split realities, a dark sea of occurrences both known and never-thought, spiralling to their nocuous conclusions.

The substance of post-Christmas week was appreciably less thrilling: Dan wanted me to come to Lachlan's for a dinner party. The novelty was that this would be a weeknight dinner, which was traditionally challenging for a salaryman to host.

I was nervous, partly about seeing Chris L but mostly about seeing Dan in this much-feared apartment, which I had not previously been invited to. I stood in Dan's empty bedroom to take advantage of his luxuriously person-height and person-wide mirror, spat in my hand and smoothed my hair. Some people shook, sweated and wet themselves when nervous, so I guessed I should be grateful that in a time of need my body unleashed only this eerie automata, this spitting and smoothing, hairstyle tics.

My youth allowance had clicked over into another fortnight, although we were entering a terrifying badland where public holidays did weird things to scheduled payments and it was both necessary and impossible to prepare for this. I walked up to Blackhearts on Lygon Street and bought a nice bottle of rosé, which was beading by the time I disembarked the 96 and descended into Fitzroy, really Collingwood, because their building was at the top of Oxford Street.

In the late afternoon light – which in summer was just daylight – the industrial façade of Lachlan and Chris L's building looked stately and warm. Balconies had been bolted to the brick exterior and residents had filled them up with green things in large pots. I buzzed in and walked to the elevator, very quickly, never having been there but at some point having learned that the body corporate was cracking down on 'loiterers' – visitors. Up here on the third floor, a large black door flung open.

'I'm so glad you're here,' said Lachlan.

I took a deep breath. 'What's wrong?'

'Dan's being unreasonable.'

'Sounds good,' I said.

Dan had always laboured under the false belief that he was wonderful at hosting, when in fact he couldn't multitask; the sight of two burners, burning low, could make him bloodthirsty. If he had to coordinate more than one cooking timeline, he was liable to snap a spoon and stab you.

But what nice drawers held the wooden spoons in this Fitzroy apartment! Lachlan had led me into the kitchen, lean and dark, and the drawers themselves were lean and dark, wide and deep and stark, a pan of tofu perched above them, bubbling.

'Hi Dan,' I said.

He whipped around and hissed.

'Shh, shh,' I told him.

'Don't shoosh me,' he said.

'Oh no. I thought you liked being shooshed.' Just like I appreciated being hissed at. I got in behind him and gave him my 'false hug', another of my privately developed specialities; I had learned to encircle people without ever touching them, with the aim of providing comfort through proximity.

It was like the awful kids' game where you have to move the wire loop to the finish point without bumping the wire track, otherwise it zaps your hand on contact. Dan kept moving around tensely and I kept adjusting, but then he settled down, as if I'd managed to push some important nerve. But he always outsmarted me – he'd just relaxed his bones so he could gain the space necessary to wiggle out of the circle, elbowing me in the stomach for good measure.

It was too soft to be categorised as true undue aggression, but too hard to be taken for a 'friendly jab gone wrong'.

Lachlan looked embarrassed for both of us. He said, 'What could be so wrong?'

And we listened to the story of how Dan had become an hour behind on his always roomy cooking schedule, because he'd needed sherry vinegar but while the Smith Street stores were more various than the ones at Barkly Square, it was less easy to know what they would stock. The fruit shop didn't have it, and the health store didn't have it, and the woman at Sonsa Foods seemed to appreciate the question, suggesting deep knowledge of sherry vinegar and its role in Dan's life, but when this knowledgeable person led him to a secret cache of vinegars, she found that someone earlier must have purchased the last one. This left Dan with the evil Coles or also-evil Woolworths. He tried one of them. 'Just one of them.' He would not say which one. There, Dan had assailed a friendly-seeming teenager in mid-vegetable-restock with requests for sherry vinegar. This teenager had asked Dan which aisle he thought would have it, and then he'd gone with Dan to visit Dan's suggested aisle, as if Dan had been asking for a second set of eyes rather than professional intel. While watching the boy hunt in the aisle where Dan knew the vinegar wasn't, saying, 'Hmm, I'm just not sure if we have it or not,' Dan had said, 'Not to be rude, but could you find someone who knows?' – causing no amazing expert to come running.

'Could you just use other vinegar?' asked Lachlan.

I widened my eyes. But Dan only shrugged and said, 'I did. I'm being unreasonable.'

For most of our lives, the interesting moments are dealt with before they are fatal.

Lachlan took my too-warm wine and poured some for the two of us, then led me to the dining room, where I complimented him on his collection of large abstract prints and red-stained wooden furnishings, everything dramatic and cosy. I had not previously associated Lachlan with objects of this kind and was both stunned by their sophistication and designerly exactness and amused by how classically male and sophisticated they were, in a way that hung weirdly off a person in his twenties, unflattering and baggy like my only suit. There was also statuary and funky twisted lighting.

'I assume it's your statuary,' I giggled. I was two sheets to the wind, having again raided our back-of-cupboard booze stock before tramming in, this time drinking a sticky orange liqueur.

'No,' he nodded placidly.

'Chris L?' I said.

'Not his,' said Lachlan.

'Lachlan's mad because Chris L won't come out for dinner,' called Dan. 'He's in the lounge room watching Foxtel.'

I was halfway annoyed that Lachlan hadn't clarified things himself and halfway fascinated that he expressed his rage towards Chris L by neutrally explaining that certain objects belonged to neither of them. I sometimes wanted to like Lachlan. But he made it hard.

'You guys have Foxtel?'

'No, we don't,' said Lachlan.

I drew out the story like a breakable thread, hand over fist, delicate.

It turned out we were in the apartment next door to Lachlan and Chris L's, which belonged to a couple, two gays, I could smell it, who had gone to the country for the Christmas period and needed somebody to look after their cat.

'Therefore the dinner,' said Lachlan.

'We have to eat the cat?'

'This apartment is three times the size of Lachlan's,' yelled Dan from the kitchen. 'Also, these people have extremely handsome stuff.'

I reached across the table to pour myself more wine and was amazed to see that two thirds of the bottle was already gone. Lachlan's glass was barely full, now it was full again.

'The other night,' he said.

'Yes?' I said.

'When you came out to the queer party.'

The last night of November. 'Yes,' I said.

'Thank you,' he said deeply. 'It meant a lot to us.'

'Oh,' I said.

He looked at me across the table.

'And when we walked away,' he said.

I arranged my face into its most neutral shape. I'd forgotten this had even been a mystery.

'It was a moonlit night,' said Lachlan.

'A moonlit night,' I said. I could picture it. Every night was moonlit.

'It was a moonlit walk.'

'Yes,' I said.

'To Fitzroy Gardens.'

'Yes?'

'To the duck pond.'

'. . . Yes?'

'Dan took off his shoes.'

'Yes.'

'And a duck bit his toe.'

I stared at him – was that it? – whereupon he leaned back and crossed his arms and looked drunkly at the ceiling, I guess disappearing into moonlit reverie.

I heard breathing and turned around, and there was Dan, standing in the throughway with an odd distant expression, lost in his own hazy late-spring memory.

He caught me looking, and I saw his little features squeeze up, willing me not to say anything or make fun of Lachlan. I nodded, because of course. I nodded twice, because I was drunk.

'That's probably enough,' said Lachlan. He nodded. 'Yes,' he said.

Neither Dan or I was stoic, and nor was my family, or anyone we'd known at uni, so I wasn't used to it, but I thought it would be a fine quality to have. To deliver things carefully, and steadily, and rarely. And then make sure to underscore the moment. But now Lachlan's reserve seemed to return from the top-secret location our personalities like to go when we're drunk, and he was looking directly at me, and I squirmed.

'Dan says you've been seeing someone,' he said.

'What? Who?' I said.

'Someone from Richmond,' he said.

'. . . Could you be more specific?'

'He drives you around.'

'Oh,' I said. I relaxed. 'He drove me one place, one time.'

'Tell me about him,' said Lachlan. His eyes were closed again. I laughed.

'There's *nothing* to say.'

'Any details,' he said.

'Ummm,' I said. If I was not used to stoic people, I also wasn't used to Lachlan suddenly craving detail of this kind. Not that I had these details, the details he implied, but if I'd had them, I would have felt weird also. Dan and I were gossipy, but we didn't really talk about other people's bodies or what we did with them. I decided to request clearer instructions.

'What details?' I said.

Lachlan leaned in close.

'You know Dan and I are monogamous,' he said.

I couldn't help but giggle again. He was sooo drunk, so was I. Another gasp from the doorway, then footsteps. I sighed.

'Would you excuse me,' I said.

I got up and swayed in the direction of the kitchen.

'Dan,' I said.

'Yes,' he said.

'A duck bit your toe,' I said.

'Yes.'

'And you're monogamous,' I said.

He put his head in his hands. 'I'm monogamous,' he mumbled. He raised his hands a little, so they weren't covering his mouth. 'Lachlan and I are the forty-nine per cent.'

I rushed up to him. 'Dan, it's good!' I said. 'It's nice to be monogamous.'

He peered out between his fingers, slyly. 'Are you *shocked*,' he said.

I rolled my eyes and turned from him, lured by the promise of the TV light, the Foxtel light, flickering down the hall, through an opening on the other side of the kitchen.

'Resist,' he called after me. 'Resist seeing it as a progression.'

'Not a progression,' I called back. 'What is it, an orb?'

I laughed to myself again when I'd got down the hall. No, it was *not* an orb. We were just drinking and talking, laughing and hanging. Now here I was in this strange room, like a bad conclusion: the TV blared massively, bright and flat and loud, and under it, a sulky shape was curled up on the couch.

'Are you okay?' it asked me. So it was not the cat.

'Chris L,' I said. 'I didn't recognise you.'

He picked up a pair of sunglasses and put them on. 'How about now?' he said.

I laughed. 'No.'

A nature documentary was cycling on the TV. Fabulous fish in violet colours and of violent nerve were darting through the water, picking up hunks of food, and then darting back into the protecting arms of a pink anemone. 'Look at these fancy fish,' the narrator was suggesting. 'These florid, fancy fish are very hungry, very social.' As if this were the exact message you'd take from the footage and he was simply narrating what any reasonable person would see.

'What's up?' I said, and plonked down in the sofa, which left a vast cushiony emptiness between Chris L and me.

'Bad things,' he said.

'Pad things?' I said, drunk. 'What are pad things?'

'Bad things.'

'Pad things?'

'Come on,' he said, and out whipped his arm – not from underneath a shawl but from a nest of blankets, which gifted him the same effect of casual surprise. A remote control was tossed at me. Because it was Foxtel, it was a substantial remote. But it was only a toss, so it landed softly, coldly.

'Sorry,' he said.

'That's okay,' I said.

'Not really bad things.'

'Cool,' I said.

He was just being teenagerly, and I guessed I also was. We sat there together, radiating malice.

We watched the screen in silence while I thought wonderingly about Dan and Lachlan, and what I could say to make Dan feel better about his life. Only he would view monogamy as a personal failing, which must make it very confusing to get the things you want. I scooched closer to Chris L, just a little closer. After that I stayed where I was.

When Dan shouted, 'Kids! Dinner's ready,' I was shocked to find that half an hour had passed without us saying anything; Lachlan must have been in the kitchen, entertaining Dan.

Had I ever spent this much time on a couch, not talking with somebody? Not with my family, not with Dan. But with this swaddled person.

I think he made me want to explore my sociability.

Appearing at the dinner table, drinking with everyone, Chris L, who had donned a shawl once he'd wormed out of the blanket, kept touching the arms of Lachlan and Dan in ways that I found to be both natural and charming, simple in their expressions of feeling and comfort. We talked about Lachlan's bank job, Dan's work at the design firm, why Chris L hadn't gone to uni – he had been born for retail – and what I would be studying at the end of summer, which were the subjects I'd saved for last, unsequenced but introductory. Chris L's hands kept darting from the folds of his cream shawl to respond to text messages, and I kept stealing little glances at his phone.

They were women's names and numbers. Who even were these women? I wondered if Chris L met these people through work, and if I should have spent more time making friends at uni before Dan graduated and took away my key social access point. It was depressing that the easiest ways for me to meet new people were hook-up apps and people who lived with people who Dan dated. I definitely had to make friends other than internet and sex people, but how would I greet a person who was neither of these things? I could talk to them about books or Dan or nature documentaries. I could go up to a person and say, 'Surprise me!'

I couldn't think of a way to ask Chris L for info about his friendships that wouldn't seem creepy ('Looks like you have some pretty interesting names in your phone') so I resigned myself to a narrow life, a joyless tomorrow. The time we'd spent on the couch was already softening into the mentossy tones of a sleepover party. A dream I'd never had, a weird shadow of memory, like brushing our teeth together at the bathroom sink.

I stayed after the meal to help Lachlan stack the dishwasher; Chris L didn't. Owing to the wine, I crashed on the couch Chris L had vacated in favour of sleeping in the adjoining apartment, the smaller place where he actually lived. This apartment I'd come to see was apparently destined to remain unseen.

If we lived in a world that was laden with poetic justice, the TV room I slept in would have shared a wall with Chris L's bedroom, and I would have been woken on the strange couch by a buzzing in the night, and Chris L saying, 'Yeah? . . . Yeah? . . . Now? . . . Are you sure?', then the sound of Chris L letting somebody into the building, then the sound of many interlocking snaps and clicks and umphs, which despite their general nature clearly belonged to Vivian – the specific person whom I did not want to have produced the sounds.

Because we do live in such a world, that is exactly what happened. I stayed up for hours on my phone with the light turned down, regretting that I'd ever met Vivian or Chris L, going through Chris L's internet photos in search of answers, wondering at the power of this unfathomable person, whom I could not respect but also could not understand. Where once I'd liked to look at Chris L's Instagram when I needed a dose of something slightly acid, like a sting, I now knew too much about him to really get involved in the drama of the silver cape, its full ridiculousness.

I tried to look at my other favourite men of Instagram, who couldn't go to karaoke or have a morning swim without it turning into a giant personal journey. They had to overcome a major struggle every day. Life isn't so full of events, you dummies. Spend a day eating macaroni, before it's too late.

But now my life, too, was dangerously close to such eventfulness; I'd come to a dinner party and slept over on a couch! And, sometime in this chapter of this jeopardous adventure, the neighbour's cat decided I was sufficiently chill. It hopped up on the couch, and then it cuddled in beside me, and then it was gone by the time I woke up.

After a while, I wandered into the strangers' kitchen, where Lachlan was pulling the leftovers from the fridge. Last night's taco filling was this morning's tofu scramble, which I could not wrangle into an arresting metaphor for the uncertainty I felt around Lachlan this morning, just from having been around him lots the night before, at which time he'd revealed himself to be somewhat different from the person I'd semi-blindly assumed he was. I sat down at the bench and smiled shyly at Lachlan.

'Stop smiling at Lachlan,' Dan said, swooping in, fresh from the shower, trying and failing to casually shrug on his dressing gown. It was the familiar one, lush with deep green pile. Even here in Fitzroy I couldn't escape it! He must have brought it with him from our house.

Dan saw me inspecting it. 'I know,' he said. 'It's too hot! What am I thinking?'

'No,' I said. I couldn't stop looking at the gown. 'I think I . . . like it?' It was almost true; after constant exposure to this robe, and also to Lachlan's, the piney, homey depth had finally seduced me. 'I *like* the robe,' I explained.

'I think I'm done with the robe,' Dan said. 'I'm leaving it here in Fitzroy.'

'That seems extreme,' I said.

'But I have to,' he said enigmatically, 'because it's not mine.'

He assumed a scary expression. I would like to say that if the outside world ever saw this expression, Dan would find himself out of work, out of friends, and out of tofu scrambles; he would have to spend the rest of his life living under a troll bridge, dining on the braver pets and dumber village children.

'What are you doing?' I said. 'Lachlan, tell him to stop.'

'Please don't make that face,' said Lachlan.

'I'll stop if you open the pantry,' said Dan.

It was such an awful face that I was genuinely frightened.

'Why do I have to open the pantry?' I said.

'Why *not* open the pantry?' said Dan.

I always lost games like these, because I didn't care, not in these cases, and you could say this was the point of the game – who can care the most? – but if you go along with it, it becomes impossible to ever quit anything and still feel as though you have made a legitimate choice. Maybe it was this, Dan's way of taking things too far, that had lent his relationship its sheen of survivability; if I could just hold out another day, another lonely weekend, their relationship would unstick from the far edge of the pan and sizzle into ether, never to be seen again. Now, with Lachlan becoming my ally this morning, this wish seemed both unlikely and cruel.

'Go on,' Dan nodded at me. 'Do open the pantry.'

'Fine,' I said. I opened the cupboard door.

My eyes were closed. 'Should I look?' I said.

'Of course you should,' said Dan.

Inside the kitchen cupboard was a wall of folded towels – bath towels, face washers, handtowels, and, of course, the dressing gowns modelled by Dan and Lachlan, my favourite couple; two rows of these dressing gowns occupied the bottom level of this floor-to-ceiling pantry. Each one of these things was the same deep green colour, luxurious and uniform and thick, thick, thick.

I turned around. They watched neutrally. 'What does it mean?' I asked.

'It's not really a mystery,' said Lachlan. 'The people who own this apartment run a towel supply company.'

'Thank you,' I said.

'And that's the towel game,' said Dan.

I frowned. 'Huh?' I said.

But before he could reply, or try to not reply, whatever, there was the sudden sound of two people fumbling at the apartment door. They made a helpless music of turning knobs and sticking deadlocks, and with everything coming together lately – ducks with toes, towels with towels – why not also these ones, porous walls with porous walls, the flimsiness of this building and the flimsiness of home. I was nastily pleased that, in this expensive apartment, everyone was still exposed to swarms of bumps and sounds. I braced myself for the arrival of their producers.

Chris L was wearing a neat pair of diamond-patterned boxers, tastefully covered in a peacock-patterned shawl, and of course his sunglasses, in this sunny kitchen. Vivian was strangely wearing white boxer briefs only, which formed a trifecta, with the swimming trunks and sweatpants, of clothing that was irresponsible and inappropriate, his dick being revealed with escalating clarity.

I tried not to see this as a progression. For the whole time since the door had started bumping and clanging, I'd been nervous to know what would happen when they both got through, whether Vivian would say something telling and salacious that made my couch friendship with Chris L seem liarly and gross. It is terrible to realise that you have something to lose, even if that something isn't much and it's new and largely based on a brief spell of mutual TV-watching. But my relationship with Chris L had extended past whatever milestone where I should have told him I'd been to Vivian's place, and now if Vivian did say something I would be found out as an unsuitable friend, false and creeping.

But I understood that Vivian would not produce such a reveal; he was obviously surprised to see anyone in the kitchen, and after looking at us, one by one, he made the decision to keep marching towards us in his briefs alone. Chris L walked straight to the fridge and pulled out a bottle of orange juice without saying hi to anyone, which I thought was kind of great because it was not his apartment, compounding the egregiousness of neglecting to warn Vivian that anyone might be here.

'Good morning, mates,' said Vivian.

'Good morning, Vivian,' we all said as one. I nodded at Vivian. He nodded at me. He looked either fresh from a shower or healthily sweaty. All of us were strenuously not looking at his underwear. Chris L poured his juice into a glass and held it to his lips and allowed his sunglasses to reflect the room's occupants back to themselves. They watched him drink the pulpy orange juice.

'What are you boys doing today?' said Vivian.

'Going back to bed,' I said.

Chris L snorted mid-drink, which made me grin at him. It was the kind of snort that said 'That's so you,' and to the room, 'That's so him,' an arena of judgement that was usually Dan's only.

'Don't go back to bed,' said Chris L. 'Come to the pool.'

I scrunched my little nose and balled my little fists. There was no way I was going to spend another day lying on those bleachers, talking shit and deepening my complicity in the burgeoning relationships of anybody. Besides, I knew just how mornings like this went – vague plans, they might end up back at someone's apartment, where the stated goal would be to play a game or see what was on Stan but they'd circle back, and circle back, and someone else was coming, then someone else was hungry, then someone had to go . . .

I wondered if I could still be a part of this circle of friends if I did not actually like spending any time with them, and also if I did not like the things they liked to do, which were somehow different from the things I liked to do, even though they weren't that different in the scheme of doings.

There are fun ways to be a bad sport, which I quickly catalogued, but I was saved by Vivian from saying any of them. 'Aussies and their pools,' he said.

This was the beginning of any number of plausible sentences, but a natural conclusion seemed not to be in store; Vivian chose to leave the statement hanging. Chris L watched him impassively. Dan and Lachlan were bored. I was just trying to keep my eyes above the neckline, which is the expected focus of all conversation partners – it was another moment where I might have slipped the bonds of fate, if I had recognised the kitchen as a deadly situation, a location where my attention could have been wisely paid.

Maybe the first relationship was with horniness itself, which was always there inside you, waiting for the moment it could fuck you up the most.

'I might come to the pool,' I said.

'*Really?*' said Dan.

'Yes,' I said. I winked at Dan. 'I'll keep you informed.'

'Great,' said Dan. 'Really good that you'll keep us informed.'

'Are you going home first?' said Lachlan. Lachlan! I smiled at Lachlan. He smiled back, perhaps a bit uncertainly.

'I think so,' I said.

'Why don't you take a towel?'

I re-opened the pantry and I helped myself to two.

All afternoon, I sent to Dan noncommittal messages and received little parcelled-out messages in return:

the couples had split off, to do whatever they wanted, then Lachlan had gone off to have lunch with a friend in Southbank, and Dan had gone into the city to meet up with him afterwards.

There were still provisional plans to have a swim, but these seemed increasingly like a collective MacGuffin. I felt sorry for the languishing employees of this pool, who'd spend the whole day wondering where all those swimmers were, peering out at the unpeopled horizon.

I stayed in my gruts, hot and slick, a damp night moving in; it kept to thirty-five but the humidity was whomping, prickly and velvet, sickening and slithering. Dan wound up at Lachlan's neighbours', eating all those leftovers; I was welcome to join them, but the details they imparted, a comprehensive ingredient list for toasted tofu sandwiches, suggested the careful construction of a cover story. Maybe they were having sex, or only making mood boards, or they'd realised that, fairy-tale-style, they'd gone too far with towel theft, taking first one, then another, then another, then another, until some moral about the commons was uncovered, the consequences mythical, the charges federal.

Dan was monogamous! And towel-obsessed! And Dan! Many housemates, many friends, blocked each other on Grindr, a gentleman's agreement that allowed both parties to be comfortably gross and constantly online, but I loved seeing his little face humming on beside me. *No thanks*. I would miss his ever-unblocked presence.

I showered first with one green towel and later with the other, grateful for the two clean presents in the humid evening, where towels slung on the balcony would just stay wet all night. I was failing all the marshmallow tests, and they weren't even marshmallows. What would they say at my funeral, once I'd had my last long shower? I imagined Dan standing at the podium and saying, 'One thing's for sure, he really tried to do as he liked.' And someone putting their hand up and saying, 'Sorry, I know it's sad, but in the interest of accuracy, don't most of us do that? Are you going to say that at everybody's funerals?'

'Yes,' Dan would say. 'I'm going to say that at everyone's funerals.'

I was so sure the day's business was unavoidably over that I wiped the benchtops and sprayed the bathroom with mould-killing spray. Dan was very tidy, but wasn't very clean – his nature just abhorred a vacuum. So I vacuumed and mopped the floors and they stayed thick with moisture. I showered and moisturised until the moisture sopped.

If you weren't careful, you could spend your whole life moisturising, and for what? I messaged my friend from Richmond. 'Hey what are you doing tonight?'

'coming to your house for sex. you?'

As before, he pulled up outside. When he opened the car door, I held up my hand in sombre greeting, serious and formal.

I hadn't hosted in a long time and I wished I could do that thing guys sometimes did, where they offer you a beer. What else did they like to do? Okay: when you got there, they moved you quickly past the doors of other private bedrooms. They played techno through their laptop speakers and they barely talked.

'Should we sit down in the kitchen?' he said. 'Or should we go upstairs?'

'How do you know I live upstairs?' I said.

He looked at me dreamily. 'Because we're downstairs now,' he said, 'and I can't see any bedrooms.'

It all checked out. I walked him upstairs.

He was looking at my bedroom. At least I'd brought my mattress back up here. If I'd been any older, this quiet room, with books and bed and blu-tacked Xiu Xiu posters and zero plants, would have looked like it belonged to the unwilling subject of a genuinely brutal divorce.

Late at night, when I was alone in this bedroom and Dan stopped in the doorway for a check-in and a chat, I could see him silently reassessing its 'neutral vibe', as if newly deciding that it was fine, fine, fine. He once left a bundle of decorative sticks on my pillow, and

I had to retaliate by leaving a knife on his to show him how spooky it was to find a thing like that, ominous and witchy.

But it was fine, fine, fine, because I was young, young, young. I flopped back on the bedspread and patted the mattress. My Richmond friend sat down and I felt a sudden, happy helplessness: where to put my hands? Who to marry? How to sit?

'What do you want to do?' I said.

He rearranged his legs. 'Anything,' he said.

He put his hands on either side of my neck, flat-stiff like ping-pong paddles, and moved them slowly upwards onto my cheeks, then quickly into the air. It was the strangest and nicest thing I'd ever had done to my face, so I moved my face towards him and hovered near his lips, in that strange pre-kissing pose of silent intent: your arms hang there, his arms hang there, your chests and legs aren't moving, as if you are giving space to the whole kissy event. I wanted to do something gross, like lick his cheek or something, but instead I breathed into his ear and pulled back when he gasped.

I took off his shirt and he unzipped my jeans, and soon our clothes were kicked together half-under the bed.

'Let me slip into something a little more comfort-able,' I said, pulling a roll of condoms out from the top dresser drawer.

'I have to tell you something,' he said.

'That's okay,' I said.

'No,' he said, and moved away. 'I have to tell you something.'

How many moments do you spend your whole life waiting for, without necessarily realising how much you want them, or how carefully you've been preparing for this exact thing? In this case, it was the fantasies I'd conducted in my head about repeating Dan's moment of disclosure, when he'd told me his HIV status and I had said, 'Whoa.' I knew that disclosure moments, like coming out moments, were to be resisted, because they reduced the lived reality of an idea and made it too much about the other person. They were predicated on the assumption of secrecy and vice, because only indecent things have to be declared in the first place. As if to illustrate exactly this – to make it about me – I was now prepared to be good at this un-meaningful thing, to receive the news with perfect grace. I nodded and said, 'Okay.'

'But I can't just tell you. I'm shy,' he said. 'I just need to feel comfortable.'

I looked at him expectantly. 'You're on a mattress,' I said.

'No, but if you sort of lie facing the floor,' he said.

I looked deep into his eyes.

'That would make you comfortable?' I said.

He nodded.

'Okay,' I said.

I got off the bed, looked at him again, then lay down on the floorboards, with my hands pressed down beside me in the baby cobra pose and my nose squashed against the naked wood.

'No,' he said, 'I sort of mean – hang on, come back up here.'

I got up, saw that he was lying face-up on the bed, lay down next to him, and allowed him to position my head on his stomach, facing not so much the floor as his thighs and underwear. 'Ahh,' I said. 'You mean not looking at your face.'

'Yeah, that's what I said.'

Silence.

'Facing the foot of the bed,' I suggested.

'I could go,' he said.

'No,' I said. 'What do you have to tell me?'

'I want you to fuck me without a condom,' he said. 'Are you on PrEP?'

I sighed. Of course I was, of course I wasn't; like everyone, I'd taken PrEP as a rite of passage, like the first time you buy cigarettes just because you can, but like cigarettes, it was costly, especially if you were never going out or having sex. I explained this to my Richmond friend, my head on his stomach.

'*Well*,' he said. 'I am on PrEP, so we can do whatever we want.'

I rolled over and faced him.

'No, come on!' he said.

'You obviously know what I'm going to say,' I said.

But he probably didn't. He probably thought I was going to lecture him on how the point of PrEP was to take your sexual health in your own hands, and for me this meant not necessarily trusting a random stranger to take the appropriate tests and have good-ish adherence. But actually, if he wound me up, I would get all nuts and rant about how PrEP could be kind of neoliberal, cruel and rude, because while everyone talked about its blue life-changing alchemy it hadn't been neg guys who'd kept transmission rates down in the years between antiretrovirals and the present. I had read stories online about neg guys in the aughts who disliked or mistrusted condoms and only slept with poz boys, because they knew they were safest with the people most likely to stick to their life-extending treatment regimes, whittling down their viral loads till they were undetectable. But you still heard about idiots who spoiled a good thing by taking PrEP but declining to sleep with poz boys anyway, when poz boys' medication was the more effective.

'You will literally not be able to tell the difference,' I said.

'It's psychological,' he said. 'You can't argue with that.'

This was dumb, because in that case, really what can you argue with? But the goal now was to come to some sort of agreement by which we could put our clothes back on with dignity intact and nobody doing anything that would reflect poorly on them later, no broken promises, no dissolving principles.

If it's on, it's not on ;-P! His profile had said this. I had thought he was being Gertrude Stein-ish, Zen and fun. I tried to make myself slow down and consider him. This person, basically nude, so different from those pictures. The way someone could end up here, a stranger and you.

I touched his hand and said, 'I have to say, I'm impressed. You have a clear idea of what you want. You're not afraid to go for it.'

'Thanks,' he said. 'I don't know, I'm just at the point where I'm done playing with men. I know exactly who I am.' He squinted at me. 'What about you?'

I moved my hands anxiously underneath my thighs. 'Are we still talking about PrEP?' I said.

He shook his head, got up, saw one of the damp green towels hanging on a hook on the wall, and wrapped it tightly around himself, his underwear and all.

'Hey,' he said. 'This is a really nice towel.'

'I know it is,' I nodded. I still didn't know where this was going.

'I've come to realise life is in the business of closing doors,' he said. 'It's the new year soon. If you're not careful, you'll – jeez. Is it really hot?'

He walked towards the sloping balcony I shared with Dan and unlocked the wonky window and clunked it open. Sudden air thumped through it, not humid, but not cool. 'Ah,' he said, and closed his eyes, and breathed in through his nostrils. 'Do you know what I'm talking about? I'm talking about the mpghhhhhh.'

'What was that?' I asked.

He slammed the window closed. 'Sorry,' he said. 'It's a bumpy night out there. I'm talking about facing up to the unknown but chosen, and still having the courage to jump in and fly through.'

I looked at him in wonder. He turned around and faced me. 'Courage,' he said. 'It is about guts. These Melbourne boys, they're all so cool. They don't know what they want. I want someone to take care of me when I'm old and dying. I want a mortgage and comfort. I love being looked after. I also really like the feeling of looking after somebody. I don't know if I like you, but you can get used to anything. I *really* want to go on a third or fourth date with someone. I *really* wish someone would just show me who they are.' He clapped a hand over his mouth. 'Oh no,' he said. 'I've messed it up now, haven't I?'

I made myself stop grimacing.

'Not at *all*,' I said.

'Oh god, oh no,' he said. He adjusted the towel and picked up his clothes and swept out of the bedroom, down the stairs and out the door, which hammered shut behind him. I covered myself in the second towel, fur-like in the humidity. I went out to the balcony and saw the car was gone.

Someone cleared their throat behind me. Dan was in his window. I wondered when he'd gotten home, and how long he'd been listening. Funny how the creaky house was suddenly less creaky when someone might be interested in listening in on you.

'That was incredible,' he said. 'Where'd he go?'

I was free to grimace lavishly. 'Into the unknown but chosen?'

'Is he okay?'

'Yes,' I said.

'*Wrong*,' he said. 'That is a false assessment. He is not okay and it's your fault. You did this to him.'

'*Dan*,' I said. 'Not now.'

'You broke him.' He laughed. 'You ruined a person.'

I sighed. 'He's nice and normal, I promise. I think he's just embarrassed because I wouldn't have sex with him. It makes you vulnerable.' I sighed again. While this was true in general, it felt like an understatement after watching this, the vulnerability olympics. He'd done it at the bar, pretending to have accidentally blurted something that he secretly wanted out there. This time, he'd gone too far. He'd taken my towel and everything.

'So you shamed a gay person. It's not hard,' Dan said. He leaned against the windowframe. 'You don't get a prize.'

'Shh,' I said. 'It's not fun.'

But it was fun, and perfect. Just a single guy and another guy gossiping about boys!

'Do you want some wine?' I asked him.

'Nah,' he said. 'It's late.'

'It's very late,' I said. I looked out at the park. A wide net, a dark deep. A place of free-growing night plants and oval-crossing strangers. But they were in the distance, and Dan was here with me.

'I'm done with men,' I said.

He climbed out and joined me in squinting into the dark.

'Maybe,' he said spookily. 'But they're not finished with you.'

PART 2

INTO THE UNKNOWN BUT CHOSEN

The difficulty of the fray
lies in making
the crooked
straight
and in making
an advantage
of misfortune.

Sun-tzu

There were men in the world, and they were not finished with me. I pictured plots and rituals, complex fibs and schemes. Madwomen in the attic, fake identities – the kinds of fates inflicted on people in all the novels, on women and, sure, maybe some Russians, so why not on me?

This wasn't how I wanted to go down. But Dan said, 'No, you drongo.'

It turned out this had been a needlessly alarming way for Dan to tell me he'd formally committed me to a New Year's adventure at a beach house to which Vivian had 'access of some kind'; unspoken was the idea that his parents owned it, just as they owned his squalid but valuable apartment in Richmond.

It turned out we weren't even going for New Year's Eve, when the house had long ago been booked by internet strangers; instead we had it for the night of December 30, and we'd drive back to Melbourne in the morning.

The next day, Dan showed me the listing on his phone.

'Ooh, inlays,' I said, hoping he wouldn't scan down towards the descriptive passage where I had learned this word eight or nine seconds ago.

'Those are very interesting,' he said.

'Really?'

'Yes.'

It was mid-century modern, full of rectilinear teak and fussy mid-century furnishings. Everything was polished, blond and red. Downstairs, a 'mess room' looked crammed with single bunk beds, each of them tucked under low ceilings, exposed beams. I pictured the kinds of parties they must have had there in the fifties: the proud host and hostess sleeping in the room upstairs, the last gin fizz after a long night on a wide deck, and then stowaway persons, descending those stairs, drunk and giggling; and nowadays, dead.

It's the new year soon, so my Richmond friend had said. Meaning what exactly? If you aren't careful, you'll get stuck being the same old you? Sadly, I could only be so lucky.

Soon I was in the back of a car, behind Dan and Lachlan, because whether I liked it or not – and for the record, I didn't – we were really doing this, the old me, the old them, presumably abandoned in the dark dream of this year – but not yet, not yet. These were significant new vistas! I had to assume this, because they were being blocked by Dan and Lachlan being conspicuously handsy in the front seats, Lachlan driving the car and Dan reaching over to angelically fix his hair. We drove mellow streets, then hectic highways, then mellow streets again, listening to a podcast on the tree of evolution, an image we could leave behind us as we sped on through: humans hadn't just evolved by passing down our genes, but by passing down the genes of things with which we shared our bodies. The human genome is, for instance, eight per cent virus, and little shreds are carried over when our selves are copied.

To the hatchback's right, the cold ocean, its uncompliant hands. We yanked left from the water and pulled towards the house, a few gravel-drivewayed streets back from the beach itself.

There was just one bedroom and, by the time I went in, Lachlan was already tucked in bed, with all his clothes on. He looked so cute and demonstrative that nobody could fight his claim, even knowing he was presumably still wearing his shoes. Of course Dan, who 'required' a bedroom, had put him up to this, but you had to admire the terminator ruthlessness of weaponising Lachlan for the purpose of obtaining, for himself, the ideal bed.

Under the house, as well as the bunk room, a rumpus room heavy with the tang of shed-grade chlorine. Vivian's parents must have been kind as well as wealthy, because they'd left the hot tub on, vinyl-covered, simmering.

I moved past it and into the bunk room, touching all the beds.

'I'll find the linen,' said a voice behind me. 'I'll make the beds.'

'No, *I'll* find the linen,' another voice said. '*I'll* make the beds.'

It was Vivian, and he stepped carefully into the bunk room past Chris L, who wore what looked like pyjamas, striped and comfortable, beneath a thin arrangement of grey tentacly fabric, possibly one shawl torn philosophically into many.

'Okay, *you* guys find the linen,' I said. '*You* guys make the beds.'

I clapped twice and went upstairs; and to my great surprise, Chris L clapped his own hands, a quick echo of mine, and followed me up there, a flappy tethered presence.

In the kitchen, my backpack; I had contributed bread. 'Bread and cheese,' said Chris L, 'I'm looking forward to bread and cheese.' He played with the nouns like they were new words to him, which was the same vibe that I was feeling – so grown-up, bread and cheese – but also troubling, because I had not brought any cheese.

'Bread and cheese,' I said, 'indeed, bread and cheese,' but tried to infuse the phrase with a special whimsy that said ah, yes, very good, these things, but not for you and me. Perhaps I could interest you in the greater noun of nothing?

'Chris L,' I said, holding the bread with both my hands. 'I forgot one half of the bread and cheese.'

'Which half?' said Dan. He swooped into the kitchen, a new habit of his, and lifted from a clutch of insulated bags thing after insulated thing: white wine and sparkling wine, pre-chilled water and Soda-Stream bottles, a nanginator – hmm – and orange juice. Lachlan wandered in. Nobody said anything and, when Dan and Lachlan had removed everything from the bags, synchronised, efficient, Dan folded the insulating bags into the cupboard beneath the kitchen sink.

'So great,' I said.

'Thank you,' said Dan. 'I know, it's like we live here.' He beamed at Lachlan, who remained stoic, but went slightly red. 'And now, the ideal reward . . . delicious bread and cheese.'

'Ugh,' I said. Dan made an exaggerated face of disappointment, and followed Lachlan into the bedroom.

'Hi, mates, what's up?' said Vivian, coming up the stairs.

'We need cheese,' Chris L whispered.

Vivian leaned in and smiled.

Maybe this was the beautiful person's version of baby talk, a sensuous shroud of whispers, commensurate with a preference for sunglasses and hand-obscuring garments. Chris L encircled Vivian, wiping and brushing his body where I would have looped without touching, and he said more words, whisper whisper whisper, into the pressed folds of the back of Vivian's shirt.

'Don't worry, beach mates,' Vivian said. '*I'll* go get some cheese.'

So responsible, I thought approvingly. A serious Vivian, more like the guy he'd seemed to be on the night I met him and less like a guy in loungey sweatpants. I wondered at the sex they had presumably been having and whether this somehow contributed to Vivian's upstandingness. Maybe it had brought out the very best in him, making him feel invested and responsible.

'That would be great,' Chris L whispered.

'It's no problem,' Vivian whispered too.

And he was right; it wasn't. It was all so nice and nothingy. Despite my tendency to fixate on the grimmer parts of fortune, and read dark presentiments into the summer nights, death was not the only thing for guys like us to get when we weren't attending our jobs, or finishing our minors, or buying clothes or burning fuel or striving to repeat the worst mistakes of our forebears. We could also stand around and whisper nothings.

'Cheers!' I said to Chris L. We were not yet drinking – I would fix that soon – but how grateful I was that the spirit of fun and friendship had super-seded, at least for now, my terrible attraction.

We went out on the deck, shawled Chris L and me, and watched Vivian march down the road, a cheese-gathering beach dad.

'It's so cool that you were whispering instructions into his back,' I said. 'Did you ever imagine having a relationship like that?'

'No,' Chris L said. But he was looking elsewhere, the unimpeachable view, the unswimmable sea, down, down, past the terracing tiers of this holiday town.

'It's too hot,' he complained.

'Aww,' I said. I disagreed. But I liked the skeleton finger Chris L was extending – poking at the perfect nature of the forced-fun afternoon. 'Are you having fun?' I asked him, seeking out more treachery.

His sunglasses bounced back at me. Alone on the deck, in the full bright of the blue, I took the opportunity to scrutinise these glasses, to try to see through them, because with sunglasses that is often a possibility. But they were very fine sunglasses: it was all skies and zeroes. I remembered he was moody, and a bit younger than me, prone to sulking in the flickering light of nature documentaries. Maybe he was the person who disliked being asked questions, and given the baking heat of the day, who could blame him?

'Do you want to go inside?' I whispered.

'Okay,' he said, and did, and curled up on the couch again – same old year, same old him.

When Vivian returned with cheese, Chris L was still on the couch, sleeping amid the quiet noise of the TV, and we lightly and quietly moved around the kitchen slicing bread from loaf and removing cheese from wrapping.

'Excuse me,' said Vivian, bumping into me.

'Sorry, mate,' he said, bumping into me again.

It made me realise how much I would relish being with Vivian during something like a military occupation, where we were required to be quiet absolutely constantly. Ideally we'd be taking shelter in a larger kitchen, and he would once again be in his undies.

Vivian and I kept looking at each other – classic person behaviour – in order to coordinate the food activity, and just when we were doing this, looking silently but meaningfully, Dan and Lachlan emerged from the bedroom and Dan said loudly, 'Sunset!'

The speed at which Chris L sat up was liquid, alarming.

'Sorry, Chris L,' Dan said.

I was disappointed in Dan for thinking I would 'move in' on a guy while my very good, admired friend was sleeping on the couch.

Dan turned off the TV on his way into the kitchen, a second presumptuous thing in quick succession.

We all moved to the deck.

It wasn't even sunset. But the clear afternoon was softening into a long coastal dusk, the edge of day smudging up against the blue of evening. Across the bay, the city tightened into a scratch of buildings, then kept on tightening till the scratch was cleaned away.

'Decking,' sighed Lachlan.

'This place is annoyingly beautiful,' Dan agreed.

I gripped my seat, feeling verrrry complicit in a gross colonial fantasy, and also verrrry happy on this deck above the bay. The winds were the temperature of the human body. Someone had brought Moscato, wicked, cool and sweet. We drank through the quiet, and through the sudden screams of cars. I closed my eyes, carried away, no effort.

I'm *done*, I thought.

I whispered, 'Are you done, Chris L?'

'What?' he asked me.

I opened my eyes. 'Aren't you just, like, done?'

His sunglasses, dull mirroring.

'Never mind,' I said. 'Dan, aren't you just done?'

'Uh oh,' he said. 'He's being romantic.'

'Dan, *you're* romantic,' I said.

'No I'm not,' he said. 'I'm tough.'

I sat up. 'You're capacious. Capacious enough to be tough and tender, both at once.'

We all looked at the sinking sky.

'I guess I am capacious,' he said.

I rolled my eyes.

'Capacious,' said Chris L.

The sun dropped like a bath bomb, colours blew through the sky.

'Why do you guys talk like that?' asked Chris L.

'Like what?' I said.

'Capacious,' he repeated.

'Oh, capacious,' I said. 'Because Dan is capacious,' I said, 'and I had to point it out.'

'Come on,' he said, and I knew what he meant.

I made sure to look at him seriously so he knew I was being serious. 'I don't know, Chris L,' I said. 'Let me give it some thought.'

Did I talk this way because it made it easier to discuss things, like the non-burning question of Dan's capaciousness-or-not, or was it just because I liked the way different language sounded, and glommed to it like Chris L had glommed onto his shawls? I definitely liked sounding smart, but everybody does; it would have been weird if I appreciated how much Chris L liked shawls but hoped he didn't enjoy the way they made him look. 'I don't even know the definition of the word capacious. We both just kind of *said* it,' I told him.

'Capacious,' said Lachlan.

'I don't know what it means either,' said Chris L.

'No but we do though,' I said. 'We can work it out.'

'Capacious, capacious,' said Dan.

'You can't really work it out if Dan keeps on saying it,' I said. 'But think about it. What does it sound like?'

So much quiet, so much dusk. Chris L pursed his lips. 'Vivacious,' he said.

Oh, I thought. 'I wanted you to say "capacity". Because capacity is how much room. And capacious means . . .'

'There's room,' Chris L said. He looked very happy, and I noticed the strangest thing: Vivian was watching us with something like a sneer. It was not a facial expression I'd seen previously on Vivian, and I felt myself shudder without meaning to.

'Capacious,' Dan was whispering, and as he whispered this, I looked up from Vivian's mouth and saw him seeing me, that he had seen what I had seen, the horrible sneer.

'Excuse me,' I said, and looked away from Vivian. I got up, telling myself an advantage of these new hangs, group things, was that you could get up and leave whenever you wanted. Rather than go through the house, I walked down the front steps, and sat down in the driveway and looked at the street.

A large gang of possibly-related-looking people walked past on the other side of the street, all of them smiling at the beach town, holidaying, dazzled. One of the younger members of the group noticed me. I smiled and waved. 'Look, Carl,' she said. Another person in the group took out their phone, waved back at me and took a picture.

'Hey!' I yelled.

The group had stopped wandering. The photo-taking person was smiling an easy smile.

'You can't just go around taking photos of people,' I said. 'It's prurient.'

'Umm,' a voice said. I looked up towards the deck. Dan had his arms crossed over the railing and was peering down at the driveway. 'What are you doing?' he said.

I looked back at the street, but the group was slowly leaving. 'Don't worry,' I said. 'I got what I wanted.'

'Cool. Are you coming back?' he said.

'Maybe,' I said. 'Yes.'

'Okay,' he said. He disappeared again. He re-appeared. 'All good?' he said.

I nodded.

'Okay, thanks for clarifying,' he said.

He drew back, then away again. I realised I was tanked, too much sun, too hungry, and Moscato, too early. Long afternoons in beach houses are fairly made for crushes, drawing deep salts from the muscles and poking at the bruise. I went into the rumpus room, experimented with the hot tub, lifting up the edge of the cover and leaning on the sides, went to the bunk room, didn't sleep, played with my phone, half-hoping Vivian would come in, hot and sneering, which I supposed I would have to treat like a bad new haircut, a moment to be loyal and encouraging.

The door opened. It was Chris L. 'Costume change,' he said.

He slung his luggage onto a different bed, next to a sports bag that had to be Vivian's; my backpack was still upstairs. He removed his grey tentacly shawl – I saw his lower back – then he quickly swapped it over with a shawl of lemon and brown.

'Come upstairs,' he said.

I still felt dizzy. 'In a second,' I said.

He shrugged and left. But after a little while, nearly no time at all, I dragged myself upstairs; I heard an R&B playlist pulsing through the floor.

When I got inside, went through the kitchen and into the lounge, Dan and Lachlan were crouched beside the coffee table. They froze.

'Nothing!' said Dan.

Lachlan had a fun mirrored tray in one of his hands, the other held a rolled-up fiver and a Myki.

'We used it up,' said Lachlan. 'We only had a bit.'

Dan did a sniffle. 'Sorry.'

'That's fine,' said Chris L, appearing from behind them. 'Here.' From the folds of his billowing shawl emerged a clean-lined wallet and, from within that, a cap-containing bag. There were three caps in there, with stoved tips and squished-in middles.

'How long have you had these?' I said.

'Ages.'

'Perfect,' I said. 'How much do I owe you?'

'Nothing,' he said.

I was still addled from the sun and drink, but the vision of a lemony thing in black-eyed sunglasses – it was too lovely and generous. My eyes began to tear.

'It's okay,' Chris L said. 'You brought the bread and everything.'

'There's heaps of bread,' I told him, dashing for the kitchen.

'Um, I don't think anyone's hungry,' said Dan.

I took one cap, Chris L took another. We offered the third to Vivian, who was sitting on the couch and looking at a Wikitravel guide to this peninsula, reading about the kinds of things we would not do in the morning, like hike to a koala sanctuary or visit a lavender farm. 'I'm fine, mates,' he said. 'Can't put things up your nose after thirty.'

'It's not meant to go up your nose,' I said.

He looked at me patiently. 'I'm fine, thanks,' he said.

So Chris L and I decided to split the last cap, which Chris L facilitated by striking the cap on the edge of his palm, loosening its contents, then carefully sliding half of the cap away from the other, really having to work at it and risk a gel collapse. He tapped out its ugly contents and divided them into two grimy shapes; I raised my finger to scoop up the grime, but he said, 'just lick it,' so I looked meaningfully at Dan and I licked Chris L's palm. Dan smiled, but he would have been slightly impressed by anything right then and wholly impressed by nothing, he was universally interested and universally registering, looking all around the house at everything at once. I scrambled for another drink to block the bitter crystals, a yellow-brown taste, chemical and twisted. There was more Moscato. It was just as icky.

It took ages to come on, and by the time it did the four of us were truly settled back out on the decking, the sun having sunk inside a glossy screen of black. Dan and Lachlan were both on a completely different wavelength, smoking menthols and edgily touching each other's shoulders, squinting very seriously at each other before speaking. They weren't really saying anything – comments on the house, comments on the furnishings – but whatever they said, it was articulate and grave.

Vivian had stayed inside, comfortable and couch-bound, happy on his laptop, just doing his own thing. Meanwhile, on my side of the deck, Chris L kept saying, 'Do you feel it?' No. 'Do you feel it?' No. 'Do you feel something now?' Cars drove past the ocean, the night came fluttering in, the very few streetlights were obscured by ragged trees.

'Oh, now I think I feel something,' said Chris L.

'Chris L,' I went to say, 'I honestly just think,' but as I went to tell him how self-defeating he was being, monitoring his feelings before they were even there, I felt a lightness circulating through my arms and veins, the space beneath my skin.

'Do you feel something?' he said.

'No, Chris L,' I said. Then the sac popped and the feeling filled me right up to the brim, and I leaned back in the deckchair, snuggly-snuggly, and said, 'Ahhhhhh.'

'Now do you feel something?' he said.

'You're beautiful,' I said.

He was magnetic. I realised, with great joy, that everything I once thought I disliked about Chris L was nothing short of a remarkable way of being. And to think, I used to scroll past all his identical photos when I needed a reminder of how bad things could get. I went back to the night we met, the parking garage in Fitzroy, the magic circle he'd drawn around him and me, prior to Vivian. Are you coming? he'd seemed to be saying. Everybody's here.

'Chris L,' I said longingly, 'why don't I ever see you in your silver cape?'

He briefly pulled down his sunglasses. 'It's only for the big moments.'

'Big moments,' I repeated.

'And the internet.'

At a certain point I looked around and we were all wearing sunglasses, all smoking the same menthols, all sharing the same deck. But there were only two of us chewing holes in the sides of our cheeks, while Dan and Lachlan were nestled in their messy, intense state.

'You have to go say something,' Chris L was whispering.

'I can't, I can't,' I said. We were huddled on our chairs, staring discreetly at the far side of the table.

'We can hear you,' said Dan. 'What do you want?'

'Please turn off that music,' I said. 'It's really not the vibe.'

It was jagged, chugging, lyricless. The smooth R&B playlist was still going inside, but they were playing their own music through a coney-sounding phone.

'We like it,' Dan said.

'Go inside,' said Lachlan.

My mouth opened. Lachlan had never spoken to me like that, but it suited his carriage, his stiff seriousness. 'You're right,' I said, but he was laser-locked on Dan, his own menthol burning down to cinders in his hand.

'Hi boys,' said Vivian when we came inside. He was on the couch, looking at his laptop.

I sat down beside him. 'Is Vivian still here?' He raised an eyebrow. Chris L laughed. 'Oh my god,' I said.

'That's my cue,' he said, and stood up.

'No, stay, Vivian,' we both whined. 'Hang out with us, come on.'

He hemmed and hawed, and moved his eyes towards his laptop screen, and I followed, and smiled in amazement. 'Marriage,' I said.

'Huh?' said Chris L.

What I had seen was Vivian reading a Wikipedia entry about same-sex marriage in Australia, its histories, legalities. 'I thought I saw,' I said, but I caught Vivian's eye, and though I was cooked, I could also be quick on the uptake. 'Nothing,' I said wittily. He closed the laptop screen.

But Chris L was off. 'Marriage,' he said. 'I can talk about marriage.' I was staring out the sliding door at the orange glows of Dan and Lachlan's ciggies. I almost missed the part where Chris L revealed his secret, that he had been married, *was* married, to a guy in Sydney.

'*What?*' I asked.

He shrugged. 'It was no big deal,' he said. They were dating when they passed the law, they did it as rebellion. Did the guy still live in Sydney? 'Maybe!' said Chris L.

We learned astonishing facts about Chris L, astonishing private details. Sydney. *Marriage*. So I talked through all my feelings about *that*, which were really all of Dan's, my inherited opinions, how we'd never see that outpouring of public support again, not for trans rights, not for Safe Schools, even from gay communities, because marriage propped up the edifice while boys in dresses troubled it, and certainly not for people who'd been locked up on an island by the same public who'd come out in droves in support of same-sex marriage.

'That's definitely my cue,' said Vivian. 'Goodnight, kids.'

'Goodnight,' I said, and felt briefly concerned. Had I said too much? But Chris L and I were quickly back to mutual fascination, getting all over each other.

I faxed in from another world, querying and digging. What's it like living with Lachlan? Not like you and Dan. What's with you and Vivian? It's casual, he said.

'I don't know,' he uhmmed and ahhed. He wasn't suddenly loquacious. But his sunglasses were off and his eyes were deep and dark. 'I don't think I care about boys, like, that much even,' he said. 'Not the way I care about clothes and work and things.'

'I *love* that,' I told him. 'No, I *love* that,' I said.

And I loved this feeling, the differences between us. I did care about boys, but I didn't care about work. I didn't care about clothes, but suspected I could do. Talking to him felt completely new, not bitchiness and argument, but short bursts, tiny words. It was a smear of influence. I *loved* that, I said again.

At one point, while Chris L was in the bathroom, Dan walked through the lounge room and shook his head at me.

'Dan,' I seethed at him, 'come and talk to us.'

'You guys are ridiculous,' he said. 'We're going to bed.'

'Oh no,' I said. 'Is everything okay?'

'Yes, definitely! We're just having different nights.'

That was for sure; he and Lachlan had spent two hours wetly making out, chittering on the balcony and feeding on menthols.

'Hey, Dan!' I called.

He came back out of the bedroom.

'What.'

'Do you know how I feel about you?'

'Nope.'

'It's love, actually.'

He kissed me on the forehead. 'You're munted, actually. Goodnight,' he said.

But I was not munted in quite the way I had been twenty minutes ago. I sighed at the highness I was quickly losing, and could feel my favourite feelings being sighed out of me.

'I'm really glad I met you,' I said to Chris L when he came back. When he told me, 'You too,' they were just exhausted words. Drugged flaws were appearing at the edges of my eyes, vaseliney columns with thumbprints along the sides.

At least we were petering out at roughly the same time. 'What do you want to do?' he said.

'I think we need an activity.'

'Um,' he said. 'An activity. Come downstairs.'

We crept towards the hot tub like a pair of sneaky spiders. I regarded the vinyl slab, heavy, even tomb-like.

'Are you sure this is a good idea?' I whispered.

'Yeah,' he whispered back.

I stripped down to my undies and so did Chris L. 'One, two, three,' I said and we hauled off the lid, managing to lift it down and keep the process slick.

He put his hand in the water.

'Uh oh,' he said. 'Feel this.'

I copied him.

'It's cold,' he said.

I put my hand in deeper.

'Is it though?'

He stared at me. 'Yes,' he said. 'Listen.' A beat. 'It's not switched on,' he said.

'Oh,' I said, 'that's true,' and felt obscurely guilty. Maybe I had played with it a million years ago, when I was tipsily moving through the house? The lid's been on. It's still warm,' I insisted.

He slid his forearm out of the water and shook it.

'I promise, it's cold,' he said. 'Do you really think it's warm?'

My arm was up to the shoulder now. 'I . . . don't . . . know,' I said.

It was time for a decision.

'I'm getting in,' I said.

'Don't!'

'Really?'

'Don't,' he said.

I slumped against the edge of the tub, feeling lost and wretched.

'We'll fill it up,' Chris L said. 'Come on, come on,' he yipped, so I ran upstairs after him.

We got to the kitchen.

'There,' he said.

There were two kettles on the bench, classic beach house excess. He filled them up and flicked them on and we watched. The first one boiled and switched off, followed by the second, like two sets of don't-walk signals clicking out of sync.

'Why are there two kettles?' he asked me.

I nodded, like, I know, right?

He shook his head. 'No time,' he said.

We carried them downstairs.

'Ready?' he said. I nodded. We poured them in the tub.

I dipped in my hand.

'Is it okay?' Chris L said.

I clambered up the sides and lowered my butt into the water, sensing as it hit me that I'd made a huge mistake. But by now my legs were in there, right up to my knees, and it seemed like getting out of the water would be just as bad.

'Should I come in?' Chris L said.

'I don't think so,' I said.

He hauled himself over the edge and rolled into the hot tub. His head went under. It came up. 'Enghhh,' he said.

I bit my lip. 'We'll get used to it.'

'Okay,' he said.

I swished my hands around the water but that

made it worse, it disturbed the lines of warmishness that had formed around my limbs.

'Stay still, stay still,' he told me.

'I'm having f-f-um,' he said.

I closed my eyes.

'Another ten seconds,' I said.

'Okay,' he said.

He got out.

We walked upstairs, slappy, sloshy, hunted in the bathroom for towels. 'This is really rough,' I said. 'It's rough and really dumb.'

He looked at me strangely. 'Why?' he said.

'This whole summer is filled with towels.'

'No,' he said. 'They have to give them back.'

'Huh?'

'They have to give the towels back to the neighbours.'

Of course they did . . . this was somehow obvious.

'Here's towels,' I said. I'd found the linen cupboard, which was not filled with perfect towels, but at least they were dry and fluffy.

I walked out onto the deck and dried myself thoroughly, hoping the warm night air would help.

Chris L followed me out. 'I'm going to bed,' he said.

'Good idea,' I said.

'You should put some clothes on,' he said.

'It's warm out here.'

'You're high again.'

I blinked at him. Really? I wasn't, but I was in the annoying part of the night where you couldn't turn it off and meanwhile the world became less fantastic and more boring.

'I'll come in soon,' I said.

'Okay,' he said. 'I won't hug you.'

On the table I found a nearly full pack of menthols, which Dan and Lachlan must have opened before they'd gone to bed. I tried to peel one from the packet and it took forever, my fingertips were numb and my vision was sparking. From inside the house, in the bedroom, the sound of nitrous whooshing. Maybe they had valiums? I kind of wanted to go in but kind of didn't. I couldn't even work out if I wanted a menthol or not, but I knew my hands had to occupy themselves with something.

We had to return the towels. I had found another mission.

I picked up my phone. I could focus on the screen for one second at a time, but if I looked too long, I forgot where I was looking. 'Hey', I wrote. The Richmond Man. I pressed send.

I tried to get my wits about me. 'Hey', I wrote again, and pressed send again. I had to get that towel back. I tried lots of variations. But none of the messages made the kind of sense I wanted them to make.

A screen door slammed. I put down the phone and walked over to the edge of the deck. Nothing. Then shuffling. Then nothing. More shuffling.

I lowered my knees to the deck, stuck my neck out, gripped the railing.

I saw a person-shape go gliding down the road.

I searched everywhere for my shoes, one of those long, incompetent searches where the wide deck seemed to harbour many shoes, but when I found them, they were pot plants and secateurs. When finally I did find shoes they were Dan's puffy white sneakers and it felt like a party that the world's thrown just for you. I knew they would fit me, because I sometimes wore his shoes, but never these perfect ones. It was a dangerous idea.

I filled a wine glass with the dregs of Moscato I found in the kitchen and padded like a pad thing down the stairs and down the road, and only when I was very nearly at the beach did I realise the shoes were still slung high over my shoulder, cowboy-style. The wine glass was in my other hand, the warm Moscato spilling. I was wearing only my jocks, wet from the hot tub.

I knew the shape was Vivian because it wore a collared shirt and did the khaki-panted lunging of the committed explorer, a bushwalking adventurer in the bayside night. He was way ahead of me, on the sad strip of grass that merged into the 'beach' of sand and dirt and scrub and pebbles, a gentle bay, the proper ocean crashing in the distance. A low cloud had dyed the sky, white and formless.

After probably not very long, he stopped and turned around.

I stopped as well, displayed myself in full wet-jocked near-nakedness. My pale chest, legs and tummy; the veiled shine of the moon. The wine glass wobbled. I dropped it. It rolled a short way. 'Oops,' I said.

'What are you doing here?' he said.

'I followed you,' I said.

He sighed at me. He looked out at the water.

I followed him out there. It was flat and very pure.

'Vivian,' I whispered. 'You miss Australia, don't you?'

His brow furrowed. 'What?'

My teeth were grinding. 'Oh, Vivian.' I raised a foot towards him, charged with welcome, rushed with lust.

'Glass, mate,' he said.

'It's fine, I'm wearing shoes,' I said.

I was not wearing shoes, and because of this detail, I felt my foot make contact with the fallen glass, and the glass begin to roll away, and my foot hold it fast. I kept stepping. The glass snapped.

Then Vivian was upon me. 'Are you alright,' he huffed.

He came as smell, and came as grass, and came as dark; it was exactly how I'd pictured, the cologne airporty and vigorous. We dropped down. I was on my back and he picked up my foot.

'I think it's fine,' he whispered.

He was holding the wrong foot.

I felt cold on the damp grass, my bare back, wet jocks. But Vivian's clothes were dry and warm. I pulled him roughly down.

He was grinding over me, through his clothes, and levering both my legs up, when a car hooned past. It threw its gold light over us, lit us up, and then we were both back in the dark.

Vivian said, 'Fucking hell,' and time became unstuck. He pushed off me, scrambled up, and stared at both his hands, like an actor about to howl into the rafters.

There was blood on his hands, which must have been from the cut. Like magic now, my injured foot began to sting and throb.

He wiped his hands on his shirt wildly. If he felt this bad about the blood on his hands, I definitely would not tell him about the blood on his lips, and on his cheek and throat, which I must have smeared up there when we were making out.

'Yick,' I told him, sobering. 'Well, at least it's funny.'

'Yeah,' he said. He adjusted his shorts. 'Do I have anything to worry about?'

I moved my leg to keep my foot off the ground, the sole was getting tender. 'Are you not on PrEP?' I said.

'Yeah,' he said. 'Not today.'

'I think you're fine.'

'Right,' he said. Had there really been *that* much blood? Maybe a little went a long way in a wet environment, where it mixed with sand and seawater and my still-wet jocks. 'Could you answer the question?' he said.

'No,' I said.

'No I don't have anything to worry about, or no you can't answer the question?'

He sounded almost angry, shrill. So unlike himself.

'No you don't have anything to worry about,' I said. Did I really want to do this? I cracked my knuckles and went for it. 'Because most people's viral loads are completely undetectable if they stick to their regimen. In fact, you're probably *safest . . .*'

He was shaking his head and blinking.

'Oh, Jesus,' he said. 'Oh no.'

I shrugged and sighed. 'You have to chill,' I said. It occurred to me, as I watched him have an honest-to-god freak-out, that crushing on an older guy was not without its problems, for with them came their attitudes, their daggier notions.

I looked out at the sea again. I felt grave and calm.

'You have to tell me,' he pleaded.

'Forget you, man,' I said.

'Hey!' I heard him yell.

But I was going, gone.

It was the new year, or close enough that I just let it upend me, the cold water, the gentle slope, then I floated out.

The bay was cold and peaceful. I floated for . . . who knows?

I was in a quiet place, buoyant, very comfortable. I was in a bed, and on my back, in outer space, and although all I heard was the lapping of the bay, I understood that he was out here with me.

Are you happy here? he asked me.

I didn't answer. I smiled.

We both lay there together in a fantasy of night, safe from time, like brothers, but not even like boys.

We have to go back soon, he said. He added, not now.

And just when I was happiest, I realised where I was. I gulped for air. I kicked my feet. I could not touch the bottom; who knew what else was out here, in the deep and dark?

I panicked and I freestyled. My hand brushed something *soft*. I screamed and swallowed water. I kicked—

and touched down.

I struggled forward, endless, leaving reams of whiffy blood.

I was waist-deep. I was walking.

I was dripping.

I was home.

I crawled up the beach panting, with my underwear still on.

'Vivian,' I called out, once. But he'd already gone.

I looked out at the water, at the surface, finless, still. I wanted to cry or something. I could not believe my luck.

I collected Dan's shoes. They were a real situation, their puffy surfaces tarnished with beachy grime and gunk.

I pissed quickly in the bushes and hopped dripping up the hill.

When I got back to the house I was both too buzzed and too tired to come to any decisions about exactly how bad the situation on the beach had been, but I knew it was a matter of pinpointing its specific badness – no argument for its goodness could be made from any angle.

It felt very late at night, but we'd really dropped quite early, and then, because we also hadn't taken very much, the whole thing had finished before the clock struck midnight.

I had plenty of time to consider all the details, turning them over and over as if that would make them change. I could not go down to the bunk room, of course I couldn't, so I stayed upstairs on the couch, trying to keep my mouth still and constantly needing to pee. I turned on the TV hoping *Rage* was on, but this was the holidays, it only felt like the weekend.

I inspected my cut every time I went to the bathroom. It was deep and tender, but no longer very bloody, clear and pinky-orange, accessible as skin. It must have been a little blood, mixed with a lot of water. Or it had been a lot of blood but the cut had been cleaned in the bay; I found some Dettol and rubbed it in, which stung and felt pointless.

I found a plastic bag under the kitchen sink and dumped the tell-tale shoes into it, bunny-eared the handles, and hid the bag carefully behind my own backpack, which had been shoved in the corner of the kitchen.

Finally, the sky rolled up and dragged with it the smell of several makes of hairdryer, malfunctioning in tandem and whirling through the world, expelling vigorous blasts of air. Birds that cawed like crows began their dawning noises. I promised myself and the world to never again do drugs, to never do anything that didn't have an off button.

I had the longest, hottest shower, tried really hard to come and, when I'd given up and was drying myself off, I sensed that someone else was awake. Socked feet and shuffled cutleries, the little sounds of someone doing lazy morning things.

I approached the kitchen but was struck shy. I could only stand at the entrance, my hand worrying the wall. It was Dan in his sleep shirt, oatmeal and rag-thin, covered by his green dressing gown, which I guess was comforting, rinsing dishes, crushing garlic, stirring mushrooms and flat-leaf parsley. His hands appeared old and muscly in the washy morning light; he looked for all the world like a resident of this home, taking intimate pleasure in the use of it.

'Hi,' I said.

He turned around.

'Oh hi,' he said.

A little worm of crystals was still snaking through my chest, catching on the edges and leaving little nicks.

'How did you sleep?' said Dan.

I ran up to him and hugged him.

'I am very glad to see you. It was a strange night,' I said.

'Okay,' he said. He patted my back. 'Stop stroking my dressing gown.'

I had been doing this without thinking. It was so soft and expensive. 'Wait a minute,' I said. 'I thought you had to give it back?'

'Oh,' he said. 'Maybe. Who told you that?'

'Chris L.'

'We thought we should, but maybe not. It's sort of optional.'

'That's good,' I said.

'Yeah!' he said.

'Can I have the car keys?' I said.

'What for?'

I stared at him.

'I don't care,' he said, and pointed at the benchtop. I scooped them up and subtly grabbed the bag of ruined shoes, which I tucked in the boot of Lachlan's car, behind the nest of camping supplies and box of random tools. It felt like I was getting rid of a body.

'Hey,' Dan said when I returned. 'Is now a good time to talk?'

'What?' I looked at the food he'd laid out on the table. 'Of course not,' I said.

There's one of these people in all our lives, the ones who ruin comedowns. They want to go to sad movies, loud and crowded sports, call their parents, call your parents, join Toastmasters. They never want to stare at walls and wash their weary faces, go to sleep and find a way to black out all the windows.

'Forget it,' he said.

I sat at the table and grabbed a fork. 'Happy new year, Dan.'

'That's tonight.'

'Just wish me well,' I snapped.

'Hmm. You're at a loss.'

'It's a great time to talk. I'm ready now.'

He looked at the fork in my hand. 'Absolutely not,' he said.

'I really want to go home,' I said. 'I don't want to wait around here for a million hours.' I knew I could not face Chris L. I definitely couldn't face Vivian. I couldn't face a plate of food. I could barely face myself.

'Wake Lachlan up,' Dan said.

I looked towards the bedroom door.

'I don't want to,' I said.

'Yes you do,' he said. I tried to protest further and it all came out as Vghhh. 'Wake him up so we can go home. Go on,' he said.

I squeezed my eyes shut to brace myself and walked towards the door. I pushed it open. There was Lachlan, curled up with a huge amount of doona covering his chest and arms, his feet and legs uncovered but hugged in very close. I had never seen a more resolutely sleeping person. I looked down at the floor, which was covered in nitrous bulbs. It was the nang apocalypse, no wonder he was tired.

'Lachlan,' I whispered.

Nothing.

'Lachlan,' I said.

He opened his eyes at me.

'Lachlan,' I said soothingly. 'It's time to take us home.'

He nodded, but stared sleepily. 'I don't want to get up,' he said.

'Lachlan, you have to,' I said. 'Lachlan, come on, bud.'

His brow was knitting nakedly, he looked confused and hurt.

'Don't cry, Lachlan,' I said. 'Sorry, Lachlan.'

I backed out.

'That was awful,' I said to Dan.

'I didn't make you do it,' he muttered. It was clear he hadn't realised how bad it would be.

But when Lachlan emerged he was himself again, our neat efficient buddy, helping me wipe the bench-tops while Dan gathered his things. We were getting out of here early, I was so relieved and impressed. Coming down in a stranger's house is the worst thing ever, and doing it so far from home would be worse by deeper fathoms.

I couldn't believe how fast Lachlan had gone from zero to perfect. Not everyone in the world was so practical and good.

'I love you, Lachlan,' I said.

'Faster please,' he said.

I nodded, and turned around, and I almost died. Chris L was standing at the top of the stairs, wrapped in a sheet, in his dark sunglasses, a hand on his forehead. His other hand was gripping the banister, like he was close to tipping over.

'Hiiii,' he said.

His hair was mussed up like a kid's.

'Hi,' I said calmly, and gave him my sternest nod. He looked so unprotected, barely moving, frankly looking hit. He moved through the kitchen like a blind thing, touching. 'Breakfast,' he murmured. 'I don't want breakfast,' he said.

Lachlan was in the doorway.

'Do you have your things?' he said.

'Yes,' I said. Dan was lagging.

'Dan,' said Lachlan stonily.

'I'm coming,' he sang.

I marched towards Chris L, held out a hand and squeezed his shoulder. I said, 'Let's hang out soon, okay?'

He stood there quiet, blanking.

'Okay, great!' I said.

So we all poured down the stairs.

'Are you ready?' said Lachlan.

'Mm-hmm,' said Dan. He looked at me. 'Are you ready?' he said.

'*Yes*,' I said.

I looked up at the beach house, but there was no one there; Chris L was in the kitchen; Vivian, in bed.

We purred down the street. Poor Lachlan was driving.

'Why couldn't he have a real beach house,' said Dan. 'With a nicer beach, with real sand and nice water so we could have a swim?'

All of us were quiet.

'Well,' said Lachlan. 'I don't know why.'

He drove on in silence.

'That's okay, babe,' said Dan.

We stopped endlessly for foolish reasons, water in single-use bottles and unchewable corn chips, and to give Lachlan driving breaks, which was fair enough. The sky kept on threatening to turn bold and bright and gold, but by the time the city could be seen on the horizon a sneaky god had loosed a mess of thick and mazy clouds.

But we were almost home, which meant it was almost bedtime, my favourite place to spend any holiday, particularly New Year's, when other kids were partying and never getting home, getting trapped in distant suburbs, having to deal with drunks.

'heyyyy :-)' came the message.

It was the Richmond Man! My guts twisted. I looked back at the message trail:

'Hey' I'd written.

'Hey' again.

And then an unsent text: 'It's a huge towel emergency.' At least I hadn't sent that.

Oh, boy. I felt terrible, but not so terrible that I was going to . . . what?

Actually, not anything, not the barest minimum. I was not going to explain the messages, or retrieve the towel. All of it was optional, so I was opting out.

'Not now bud,' I messaged back.

'I'm ready now :-)' it said.

'Ugh!' I said out loud.

Lachlan squinted in the rear-view mirror. 'What's happening?' he said.

'It's the guy from Richmond,' I said.

'Oh,' said Dan, 'the Richmond Man.'

'That sounds like the Somerton Man,' said Lachlan. 'Is he okay?'

'See?' said Dan.

I explained that I had sort of messaged him when I was high, strange messages that I had meant as opening salvos in a campaign that would result in the retrieval of the towel, before I'd learned the towel return was optional.

'You have to go over,' said Dan.

'*What*,' I said.

'Ah never mind,' he said.

We drove in silence.

I closed my eyes.

'No, go on,' I said.

'I guess I'm getting soft,' he said. He chuckled, amused with himself. 'I just think if you *can* be nice to somebody, you should. Don't you, Lachlan?'

'What? Sure,' said Lachlan.

'He seems so sweet,' said Dan. 'Would it be *so* terrible to, like, "go to him" and see what comes out of it?'

'Yes,' I said. It was generally true, but specifically stupid. Dan was not considering any of my particulars, like how tired I was, and how I didn't feel like it, and without these particulars it became one of those things that seemed just and good only if you weren't the one who had to go through with it. 'I miss the old Dan,' I sighed. Sleepy, sleepiest.

'What do you miss about him?' he asked.

'Uncompromising. Formidable . . .'

Vrrrrrrooooooooooooooommm.

'Wake up,' a voice said.

I opened my eyes. Lachlan was craning his neck over the front-seat headrest. 'We're here,' he was saying. The car was stopped. 'It's time to go.'

I blinked and stared at him. 'But I don't want to,' I said.

I looked around, trying to work out details and location, and opened the door slowly – 'yes, that's it,'

Lachlan said – and stepped onto the footpath – 'very good,' said Dan – and closed the door behind me. Purr and zoom, and they were gone.

If they'd died on the way home – just as an example – my last image would have been of Lachlan staring grimly ahead while Dan looked back at me with a gleeful expression, at the goodness he'd released into the world via his agent, me.

They'd dropped me off in Richmond, actually only a short walk from the stranger's building. It seemed like I should probably just get it over with.

'I'm almost there' I texted.

'good stuff :-)' the message said.

I waited for a long time under the blotty sky. The road was very busy, New Year's Eve and just past lunch. I sighed up at Vivian's, where the window was shut and the suggestive curtains were tucked neatly behind the glass. My foot hurt, but it was fine. 'I'm just downstairs,' I texted.

He buzzed me up. I caught the lift. 'Are you on PrEP yet?' he asked. He wore a stripey jockstrap and a pair of stripey socks, pulled high.

I shook my head. He threw up his arms.

'Are you kidding me?'

'I'm so sorry,' I said. I crawled into his bed and pulled the doona over me; it was much nicer than my doona, thick and deep inside.

'Lie down with me,' I said.

'Get your shoes out of my bed,' he said.

I moved my feet off the side of the bed. He came over and crawled in.

His breath was furry poison. 'I've been drinking all morning,' he said.

I moved my face away from his. 'That's pretty cool,' I said.

'You have to,' he said. 'It's New Year's Eve and everything.'

I moved further away from him; too human, too hot.

'Why would you come here?' he said. 'Do you like playing with men?'

I guessed I did. Maybe *this* was my kink, just being a bad person. I wondered if this was listed in the global index of kinks, or if it comprised a range of more indexable specifics.

'I'm actually non-dating,' I yawned.

He propped himself up. 'You're just having some me-time.'

'That's right.' I smiled sleepily. 'I'm just taking a little time to look out for me.'

I closed my eyes. When I opened them, I was alone in the bed. Unlike in the car, when I'd been ripped from sleep by Lachlan pulling over, I felt bright, revivified. It could have been hours. I stretched slowly, and got up slowly, and peered out of the bed. My Richmond friend was sitting fully clothed at the kitchen bench.

'Hello. You have to go now,' he said. He was looking at his phone.

'Okay,' I said. I walked for the door. I stopped. 'Look. For what it's worth —'

He looked up at me. I stopped.

'I'm not *trying* to mess with you,' I said.

His expression softened. 'I realise that,' he said. 'As I said the other night, you have no clue what you're doing.' And he was working himself up again, his hands becoming animated. 'You guys think you're all so young, but you are not that young. Life is now, not later! It matters! It's a privilege!'

I couldn't stop laughing. 'Stop. Who are these guys?' I said.

'You!'

I think I was meant to see him as a pathetic person. In fact, he was just pursuing his own variety of interest and seeing if anyone wanted to join in. His kink was perhaps vulnerability, performed vulnerability, although in this world it played as a kind of madness. I also knew this was sort of a lazy reading of him, because in fact it was twisted, which meant it was special. And if it was special, wasn't it honourable too?

I still didn't particularly want to spend any more time with him.

'I think I know what I'm doing,' I said. 'We just want different things.'

He studied me. 'My god,' he said. 'You don't want me. You want *him*.'

'*Dan?*' I said. I rolled my eyes. Speaking of lazy readings.

'You love Dan.'

'Whatever.' I shrugged.

In a way it was true, but not in the way you could sit there at the kitchen bench and accuse somebody with. I loved Dan like I loved Vegemite, more than that even, but not in the way that you would dress up in a jockstrap and bury like a secret.

'I didn't think you'd say yes,' he said.

'I didn't,' I said.

His eyes widened. He looked so hopeful.

'Oh, but you're right though,' I said.

He bit his fist. He said, 'Then you know where you should be.'

I liked that this was also true, but not for the reason he believed.

I had fifty in my wallet and twentyish in the bank, both of which were meant to take me through to my next Centrelink payment. Le sigh, I would have to spend; I conjured up an Uber.

Even though it was New Year's Eve, a purple dusky hour, the traffic snarl had cleared. The trip was propitiously not surge-priced. The adrenaline was pumping as I waved goodbye to Richmond. The wind had picked up again; the curtains streamed after me, making the whole suburb seem abandonable and lonely. I realised I had failed in my only mission, a towel retrieval mission. But it was too late to turn around.

'Are you okay?' asked the driver.

'Yes,' I said.

We swung left onto Johnston.

'I'm a little quiet tonight.'

'That's fine,' the driver said.

Now we were on Nicholson Street, where so recently I'd been in the car with the Richmond Man, driving in the opposite direction . . .

'Just a busy day with work,' I said.

'It's no problem at all.'

The driver pulled slowly onto Brunswick Road, then circled towards our house.

'Hey, have a nice night,' the driver said.

The car slowed down and stopped.

In my pocket, my phone buzzed.

I got out and picked it up.

It was an unknown number.

'Hello?' I said.

'Hiiii,' it said.

It was Chris L.

'Hi Chris L,' I said. 'How did you get my number?'

The driver pulled away.

He said, 'I have to ask you something.'

With keys in hand, I closed my eyes. I tongued my tattered cheeks.

'Sure,' I said.

'Is Vivian with you?'

I opened my eyes.

'What do you mean?' I said. 'No.'

I slid in my key.

'Where are you, Chris L? Are you at home?'

'No,' he said. 'I'm at the beach.'

'After *checkout*?' I said dumbly.

'All his things are here.'

His voice was crackly, ghostly.

'That doesn't make any sense,' I said. 'Is the car still there?'

'Yes,' he said, 'it's my rental. I don't know what to do.'

'Do you have his parents' number?'

'No,' he said. 'Can you come back here?'

I shook my head, of course not. 'I don't think so,' I said.

'I don't want to be alone here!'

I shook my head again. 'No,' I said.

'I don't know what to do,' he said.

'Chris L,' I began. And then the door yanked open from the inside – the key in the lock, my hand on the key.

It was Dan, and he had one of those towels wrapped around his waist, with another wrapped around his hair. 'Hello,' he said. 'Please come inside. What are you, a fishmonger?'

I looked at my phone. I'd hung up, or Chris L had.

'Because fishmongers spend lots of time loudly talking outdoors,' he said. 'Anyway, I'm glad you're here. Follow me.' He marched upstairs.

I followed him up, zombied, and he sat on the edge of his bed.

'I missed you today,' he said. 'Happy new year. Sit down with me.' He tightened the towel around his waist and patted the side of the bed.

'It's not even the new year,' I murmured. But I did as he said.

'I keep wanting to talk to you.'

I stared at the phone in my hand.

'Okay,' I said.

His hand on the bed. I looked at it. Where I was meant to be.

'I'm moving in with Lachlan,' he said. 'Isn't that exciting?'

I dropped the phone.

'Very cool,' I said.

And strangely, I was dead.

PART 3

THE NATURAL CONCLUSION

You held out your hand for an egg, and fate
put into it a scorpion.

Charlotte Brontë

I was sitting very straight. My chest was turned towards him.

I told him it was wonderful.

'That's wonderful news,' I said.

It was another automatism; I did not choose to speak. But I told him I loved Lachlan, and Lachlan was a catch, and everything would be just fine, and did I mention – Lachlan?

My blood was racing, and I knew my face was bloody-red, but I will always be proud that, in this most horrible moment, I borrowed some adult composure from Dimension X and managed to express only my absolute supportiveness. If I hadn't said what I said – he's your Lachlan, I enthused – it's likely that our friendship would have ended there and then. I was not used to pulling my weight, but it turned out I could do so in a moment of danger by repeating a single word: Lachlan. Lachlan, Lachlan. I was babbling, agreeing. 'It's my friend, your boyfriend . . . Lachlan!'

'I know his name.' Dan was laughing. 'Steady on,' he said.

He closed his eyes, his mouth twisted in soft bows, pleasure lips.

'Thank you,' he said formally. My hands on the bed twitched. Now he was holding them; they seized and squeezed his fingers. 'Ow, no,' he said. 'But thanks. Do you actually like Lachlan?'

'Yes. I didn't used to.'

'I know that,' he said. 'What are you doing with your hands?'

They'd rictussed into pincers. 'Not sure,' I said.

He shook himself off, animal. 'I think I should go,' he said.

'*Now?*' I yelped.

'Yeah,' he said. 'It's New Year's Eve.'

'Where are you going?'

'Some party in the city.'

'Yuck.'

'With work people,' he said. 'On a *rooftop*. The *Paris* end.'

'Oh, yuck, Dan. Wish I could go.'

'Make sure you go somewhere,' he said.

I blinked at him. 'I will not.'

I was all just runny organs, soaking wet and barely there.

He put on his socks, looked at his shoe rack, went hmmmm. It was fascinating: something was missing, but which shoes were gone? He did not yet know. His attention moved along before he could make the discovery. 'Why don't you call Chris L and see what he's up to?'

This was the part that set me off, a swirl of tangled images, a silver shawl, a drowned body with dark holes in the skull, a shark fin that I never saw, sex I didn't have. I gripped the edge of the bed and hung my head and howled.

'Are, you, living, with, Chris, L, too,' I gulped.

He rubbed my back till I stopped sobbing. 'Calm down,' he said. I looked at him. He shrugged. 'That's a whole other conversation,' he said.

'You *are* living there,' I gasped.

I pictured the three of them living in that Oxford Street apartment, the apartment I'd never seen but only heard through walls. This seemed almost exorbitantly awful, like my fate was both exciting and redundant. Resist, I thought. Be cool. What's at stake here? Only *everything*. Only your whole friendship with Dan. Think of something to say.

'It'll make your rent cheaper,' I offered.

'Yeah,' he said, now pulling on his clothes. 'Hey, I *really* have to go. But we can keep on talking.'

'You mean you might not do it?'

'No, that's not what I meant,' he said.

'Gotcha,' I said.

I sat there on the bed. He grabbed a pair of silver Cons and rifled through his jewellery drawers.

He whipped around and pointed. 'What are you *really* thinking?' he demanded.

'Dan, you can't ask that.' This was one of the worst things you could ever ask anybody, especially when combined with whipping around and catching them out, because nobody was ever thinking something they were meant to. 'I'm going to close my eyes for a while.'

'Um, okay,' he said.

I could hear him breathing, and then I could smell his breath.

'Thank you for being so good about this,' he said.

I nodded.

'It was only a matter of time,' he said.

I shook my head. He sighed.

'Could you open your eyes?' he said.

I blurted, 'We just live really well together.'

'Because we give each other lots of space and respect each other's choices.'

I opened my eyes. 'Yes!' I said. Finally, he got it.

'And I invite you to follow that to its natural conclusion.'

I gasped. He laughed. I shook my head and squeezed both of my kneecaps. I bit my lip and vibrated and gripped my bones and sniffed. I had to think of something to say, and finally I said it:

'There are no natural conclusions,' I said. 'There is no such thing.'

He threw out his hands. 'And I'm moving out anyway. So that is where we're at.'

I groaned and lay back on the bed.

'You'll be fine,' he said.

'Tell yourself whatever you want. Nothing that troubles the conscience.'

'Ugh,' he said, and left.

I knew I was in Dan's bed when I woke up; the linen sheets, the sense of safety; no strange smells, just comfort. I could feel my foot was healing. I knew Dan was moving out, and felt this loss and terror. I knew as I woke up more I'd feel it more acutely, but for now, in these softest sheets, I could look at it front on, maybe even live with it, the tearing of the flesh.

I stretched my back, had all my limbs. I rolled over to check my phone. It was two a.m., the first of January and, like in a dream, the phone started vibrating the second I took hold of it. I startled and I dropped it. When I picked it up again, I saw I'd missed three calls, again from an unsaved number, so it wasn't that mysterious; I'd been woken by the calls.

They rang again immediately.

I answered.

'Yes,' I said.

'Hiiii,' the voice said. Public noises in the background.

'Happy new year, Chris L,' I said.

'I drove back by myself. Can you come and see me?'

I touched my cheeks, awake and there. 'Chris L, it's after two.'

'So you can't?' he said.

I rose from my rest, I glided from the bed. 'I think I can,' I sighed. 'Chris L, where are you?'

He was the only guy in town, or the only guy at the bar, but when I left the taxi I could only stop and stare: Chris L was wearing a crisp linen collar, the silhouette of Vivian. The effect was bewildering.

He was sitting at an outdoor table at Kent Street, a bar on Smith Street, and at the sound of my footsteps he swivelled on the seat.

'I'm just wearing his clothes,' he said. 'None of mine were clean.'

He wasn't wearing sunglasses and he looked babyish, defenceless.

Along with wallet, keys and phone Vivian had left a full sports bag in the beach house packed with holiday clothes.

'Chris L, tell me everything.'

'There's nothing else,' he said. 'How good was last night, though?' He kept nodding and grinning. I realised it was the smile of the hysterical, the desperate.

'Totally good,' I said.

He gripped a sweaty beer.

'Did you check out his apartment?' I said.

Chris L said, 'I don't know where he lives.'

I thought of Dan's two kinds of men, the leavers and the leavings. Had Vivian left Chris L? Oh, of course he had. Although dyads were dyads and not essential truths, it remained the case that there were person-alities and people, and I could tell that Vivian was a leaver through and through. You're restless. You are an explorer. Things have not quite gone to plan. You are a classic *scumbag*. You march off in chukka boots.

'There's also these,' said Chris L. From down below the table he fished up a pair of boots, which were dark with fluid, and he slopped them damply between us. 'I found them on the beach today. They're Vivian's boots, right?'

My gut felt like a sour balloon, full of animal imminence.

'Oh no, Chris L,' I said. 'I think we have a problem.'

'And everybody left me!'

'Have you called his parents,' I said.

'They weren't in his phone. Here,' he said. He picked up Vivian's phone. He unlocked it – how intimate – and handed the phone to me.

'There are just two numbers,' he said.

'Right,' I said.

I looked at the phone.

I looked down at the table, between the boots and the beer, like there was something more to see than woodgrain and nothing.

'I mean, when did he get your number?' he said conversationally.

There was Chris L's name, then mine; two options to choose from and nothing in between. Why were there no parents, friends, no pizza places, nothing? What was he, a dealer? A spy? The Somerton Man?

'I'm not sure,' I said lightly. 'Did I give it to him when we were high?'

'No,' he said, 'I was there the whole time.'

'Really? You were pretty high.'

'I know where I was though.'

'Yeah.' I nodded and looked at the phone again. Those were some pretty interesting numbers he had there.

I was stuck on a detail. 'Oh my god,' I said. What hangs limply in the afternoon but by dusk billows free?

Vivian's gauzy curtains. His window had been closed when Dan and Lachlan dropped me off in Richmond after lunchtime but, when I'd left that evening, the curtains had waved after me. Hadn't they? I tried to picture it . . .

'Chris L, do you trust me?' I said.

'No,' he said.

'You're meant to say yes,' I said. 'You're just in shock. I have to get you home. Here.' I drank the rest of his beer for him, warm and displeasing, stood up, lifted his arm until he followed me to a standing position. I picked up the wet boots and handed them to him, he collected them in his arms, then I scooped up Vivian's wallet, keys and phone and shoved them in my pockets.

When we got to Chris L's place, which was just a street away, he looked pale and soft the same way as he had at the beach house yesterday morning. I wondered if he'd managed to get very much sleep. I wondered if he knew about Dan's plan to move in with him, which I had a bad feeling about, and knew that he should too. I knew it could not work, sharing a place with Dan and Lachlan. He'd be pushed out by February. Poor Chris L. I saw it all.

He did not trust me, and in fact he could trust no one. 'Will you be okay upstairs?' I said. I knew that Dan and Lachlan would not have made it home yet.

He took a step forward and kicked me.

I stared at him.

'Ow,' I said.

He looked stunned by his action. 'Sorry,' he said.

'That's okay, Chris L,' I said.

I backed away and left.

Every traffic light on the way to Richmond had it in for me and this taxi. We stopped and started, chugged and stopped, I watched the meter rise. It finished at a dollar under the amount I had, so I was screwed until payday. But I'd made it, I was here.

I left the cab.

My phone buzzed.

'WHERE R MY SHOES.

DAN.'

Not now. I was panicking. 'I have them now!' I wrote.

Another buzz; it was a picture message of the plastic bag, torn open, gutted, with the awful proof laid bare.

'Wow! Where did you find them?' I texted.

'IN LACHLAN'S BOOT,' Dan texted.

'Sounds like Lachlan has some explaining to do,' I wrote. I knew this would only make things worse, but I had other problems to deal with.

I looked up at the apartment. Windows open,

curtains out. No sound and no billowing. But I had been correct.

I thought about yelling, but looked warily across the road at the blank hull of the stranger's silvery apartment, where everyone was sleeping, maybe the stranger too.

I remembered that it didn't lock, Vivian's downstairs door, so I ran inside and up the stairs. I knocked for him; knock, knock.

It was definitely the right door.

'Vivian,' I said.

Nothing.

'Vivian!' I called.

Footsteps?

They were not.

I leaned against the door, my back to it, and slid down towards the floor. I had no money. Dan was out, and also in a shoe rage. I couldn't walk home to Brunswick, wounded foot or no.

Otherwise . . . my mind went to its most depressing places. What lunged boldly through the evening, and perhaps had drowned by dawn? He'd swum after me and not come back. I knew that's what had happened. I'd killed Vivian, or manslaughtered. And Dan was moving out . . .

There was a click and shuffle and the door drew slowly open. I grabbed at the doorframe to stop myself from falling in.

A tall figure stood over me, staggering and moaning.

'Vivian?' I whispered.

The figure stumbled back in.

'Vivian,' I repeated.

I stood up and reached for him.

But before I could touch him, he groaned and fell face-forward – a dreadful sound, meat-like as he thudded to the floor.

There was nothing to do but haul Vivian towards the next soft surface, which happened to be the couch where he had once so louchely lounged. I did this in the darkness, and so I was surprised to find his armpits soaking with a strange-smelling fluid; when I'd gotten him onto the couch, and smelled the back of my hand, I knew it wasn't seawater, and nor was it sweat. It smelled of human origin and it could not be un-smelled.

It remained in my nostrils as I rifled through his kitchen, found a clean tea towel, filled it with ice from the freezer, and returned to the couch to lay this twisted bundle on his head.

As I mopped Vivian's clammy brow, he became suddenly conscious. 'You . . . saved me,' he panted. 'You carried me upstairs.'

I imagined finding him on the nature strip, dragging him upstairs, realising how hard it was halfway through and leaving him for dead.

'Yes Vivian,' I told him. 'All the way upstairs.'

Where's your family, I wondered. Vivian, who's your Dan? I hoped he had someone who'd take him all the way upstairs, even though this sounded like a metaphor for death. Maybe this was what happened when you were fun and international, your friends drifted away from you, your parents expressed their love through access to apartments and beach houses and that's it.

His mouth swam an unusual smile; I felt tender towards him. But the smile kept going, morphing, sick and slack, and he began dry-retching, hoo-ork, until sick dribbled out.

'It's just a little,' I said, wiping it with the cold tea towel.

'There's more where that came from,' he said miserably. 'The bathroom,' he said.

I found the bathroom, found a mop bucket, ran back, put it down. Just in time, just in time.

What had happened to Vivian?

I emptied the mop bucket, rinsed and returned it, made sure his airway was clear, found a ratty blanket and yanked it towards his chest. I did not remove his soaking clothes because that seemed somewhat personal, especially after everything that happened on the beach.

I went into his bedroom and closed the door behind me. Through the only window, early light was shining in.

I called Chris L.

'Hi,' he answered.

'He's alive,' I said.

'Wow, that's great. Can you hang on?'

'Okay,' I said.

He called me back on FaceTime. He was in bed, in a room, with the golden light of a bedside light, or a desk light, all around him. He was not wearing his sunglasses. His eyes were very clear.

'I want to say this simply,' he said. 'I know what you did.'

'Oh!'

Even without the sunglasses, he gazed at me impassively; those were the eyes the whole time, the ones taking me in. They did not look particularly sharp, or particularly scrutinising. This was hardly comforting, because I had still been seen.

'Aren't you going to say something?' he said. 'You are just the worst.'

'It wasn't me,' I said. 'It was the summer.' But he'd propped up the phone and moved away from it, so I was blabbering at the wall.

When he came back a second later he had his sunglasses on.

'Chris L,' I said. 'What are you wearing?'

Then I got it.

'*No*,' I gasped.

It was the silver cape, the one he saved for the big moments. He had its edges in his hands, ready to draw it up.

His glasses stared impassively.

'Don't do this,' I said.

He yanked the cape over his face, a blinding flash of silver. He dropped the call, and I understood that my time with Chris L was over.

I looked at Vivian, sleeping, snoring.

'Stupid Vivian,' I said.

The sun was up, but I needed rest; I lay down on his black silk sheets, so bad for summer weather, but I fell asleep in them anyway, and when I woke up it was evening.

I got up, checked the vomit bucket, found that it was full, emptied it in the toilet, rinsed it out and brought it back.

The sky was like a low boat filling with the long night's water. Vivian was fast asleep, his feet sticking out from underneath the threadbare blanket, looking toe-tagged. I rooted through more of his cupboards and found some cans of beer. I filled a glass with ice and then I poured the warm beer over it, snacking on the freezer-hardened ends of frozen bread.

Sometime in the night the city underwent one of those awful cold flashes that come even in January, reminding you the bad seasons have never really gone, they can hurtle back pretty much any time they want, just when you thought it was safe to go back in the water.

Through the rattling windows I heard the cold rain settle in. It woke me, I'd been dozing, and I went out to the couch to check on Vivian again. When I looked, I saw that there was damage on his skin; it looked a bit like bruises, hyper-coloured, deep.

But nothing dark or terrible was happening on his skin. It was just the storm, its shimmering. It was just a listing tree, splashing his sleeping body with reflected, wavy leaves.

The morning sky was drenched with grey, the streets were wet and rubbished. Richmond had sunk to the bottom of the Yarra and been spat back up, a sickly, swallowed swimmer, something you could half-digest but didn't want to keep.

'Ugh, Vivian,' I said, but with a high song in my chest, because you feel in these mornings like the baby of the world, with soft bones, very tender, everything clear and sharp.

I took coins from Vivian's wallet and crept through the yuppie streets, sure that I'd run into my friend the Richmond Man, when all I wanted was a creamy soy coffee. But I was safe, I didn't, the only people here were identical couples, all wearing athletic gear, all holding their own coffees in disposable cups, all walking the same dogs. It was cheery, very Stepford.

Vivian rolled over as soon as I came back in.

'Vivian!' I said.

'Water,' he croaked.

I filled a glass and brought it to him.

'Last night,' he whispered, gulping.

'Yes, Vivian,' I said.

'Your body came out of your body and crawled across the floor.'

'What?'

'Your body,' he said, 'came out of your body, and crawled across the floor.'

My blood chilled.

'What do you mean?' I asked him. It was sick, a

possessed image. 'Oh Vivian,' I said. Those eyes, their woozy lilts.

He fixed them and grinned up at me. 'No, I'm fine now. Happy new year.'

I frowned. 'Not a nice joke,' I said. It was too close to real life; in weird of night, the weird of life, it happened all the time, part of you getting fed up and crawling out your ears.

'You're funnier when you're dying,' I said. 'You should've seen yourself.'

'Thanks for looking after me,' he said. 'How long was I out?'

'Twelve days.'

His words died on his tongue.

'Two days,' I said. 'Two.'

'Even so,' he said. He squinted. 'Wait a minute. Why are you here?'

I went to answer, but had no words.

'Do you like me or something?' he said.

I stared back at Vivian.

It was a mad question.

'Get in the shower,' I said. 'You look like a corpse.'

'Okay,' he said. He got up and ambled towards the bathroom, leaving hollow shapes and dark patches where his limbs had lain.

Did I *like* him or something? Just the opposite, nothing but contempt for Vivian. The crush was out of my system. It was a whole new year.

I heard the shower turn on. It would be the perfect cover. I could sneak out and keep going. Back to Brunswick. Back to home.

But if *that* option was so amazing . . . why was I still here?

I was contemplating my situation when he came back into the room, his own towel wrapped around him, waiting for the shower to warm up.

'You're not going to disappear on me, right?'

I was perched on the edge of the couch.

'I'd *hate* that,' he said emphatically. 'I'd feel very alone.'

This was not the kind of request that I was used to fielding. Imagine that: someone who wanted me to stay *in*.

I don't think he knew what he was asking.

That first night, after getting into the bed with Vivian, I lay there for a full minute before going 'nope!' and crawling right back out again. Instead, I slept on the couch where Vivian had convalesced through those early nights of January, sinking into the dark patches he'd left on the cushions, drawing the same ratty blanket over my legs.

I woke the next day unmolested, which was for the best, because I was not sure about the question of consent – and also of context – after what I'd said following our bloody beach-side make-out, the lie-by-omission and all its slippery implications. I went into his bedroom and was relieved to find him still not dead, breathing normally, with his paws folded over the top of his silk sheet. I walked back out to the couch, put my hands on my knees and sat, a perfect, terrified and respectful guest.

Vivian went out shopping and came back with supplies, including coffee, because the apartment included an AeroPress. He made it black for both of us and we sat down at the bench. I looked at his arms. I found I was completely uninterested, with nothing to say to Vivian, nonverbal as a dog.

'Is this okay?' I asked him. 'Not talking?'

He looked at me handsomely.

He said, 'It's *lovely.*'

It wasn't even a reading space; it was just a space to stare at Vivian and feel dread.

I wondered if Chris L had always known I'd visited Vivian, if he'd known all along my number was the only other one in Vivian's phone. Had he seen us grinding on the beach that night or did Vivian tell him – thinking it was no big deal, they were only casual, and to him we were barely summer flings before he returned to America?

I understood the real problem. It wasn't about *him.* Chris L thought he'd made a friend of me, and I had hurt his feelings. He was guarded, in some ways like me; he didn't make friends easily and, in this way, I just might have been valuable to him. It was unsayable, because vulnerable, but not unthinkable, and once I had thought it, everything made sense.

What else could make Chris L act so theatrically vengeful – more vengeful than Dan would have been if I'd indeed died out here? I pictured the way Chris L might have enacted his scheme. Vivian had woken up just after we'd driven away from the beach house, whereupon he and Chris L would have checked out and come home too. It would have become clear in the car that Vivian was sick, struck down by a summer cold; Chris L had deposited him here in this apartment, dipped the boots in water, taken his wallet, phone and keys, and called the idiot, ready to put on an act of desperation.

All of it was mostly without permanent impact. I had returned Vivian's possessions, sans the boots, and even Vivian's health had quickly been restored. But the lack of lasting outcomes only proved that it was 'something personal', a dramatic act that had been staged just for me.

Now that Vivian's health had returned from its own vacation, he turned into the ultimate, most careless version of him. It did not occur to Vivian to ask why I had come here, beyond the minimum interest when he'd first woken up. Of course I had come here, because I was, yes, a dog. And Chris L was meaningless; he'd been excised from history. We didn't talk about him, or actually about anything, and, for a few days, it seemed as if there would be no reckoning.

My first days in Richmond were embarrassingly mouse-like. My main interests included being near the walls, scaring at human noises and jumping at shadows. Our Brunswick house was noteworthy for the creaky ease with which you could tell if somebody was home; but sharing this one-bedroom apartment with a jobless holidaymaker made me realise exactly how seen I could be, a state that I found personally revolting. Whenever Dan peered at me I felt so scrutinised, which was the point of peering, or at least one of the points. But we had coexisted like this within a privacy that was built from respect and decency and bemusement, a distance eked out mutually, maintained invisibly. With Vivian there was no such careful balance.

I had always thought my ideal boyfriend would be found in a hard-to-reach location, large and silent, mythical in several important ways; which is not to say I hadn't ever wanted my own boyfriend, only that I'd wanted a very particular type, someone who required little honesty, no watering, had much tolerance for showers, maybe money, nothing else.

But it was hard to be with what amounted to a

hardy, middle-distance boyfriend, like that creature that lives in the space where the bridge of your nose should be. I would have traded anything for sunglasses and a shawl, but the termination of my burgeoning friendship with Chris L seemed to void the acceptability of copying his fashions.

I moved around Vivian's apartment, keeping a safe distance, going into the kitchen when I wanted to find food and lurking near his phone charger when I needed a hot recharge. He tried to talk to me sometimes, and sometimes he ignored me, lounging on the bed the way he'd once lounged on the lounge, where he'd later languished, and where I now snoozed.

'I just want to make sure you feel safe and comfortable,' he said.

I nodded and smiled at Vivian very carefully. If you polled a random group of hungry vertebrates, most would agree they liked their food to feel safe and comfortable. I knew I was in a lucky space, rent-free and unquestioned, but I was tired by afternoon in ways I never was in Brunswick. It reminded me of my earliest, perhaps most vicious hangovers. I kept looking in the mirror and being surprised that I didn't have a sudden bank of muscles, grossly toned. I was seething, frantic, not happy, not knowing what to do. It was a type of nightmare, my new life in Richmond.

———

I thought for a long time about the first text I should try on Dan, now that a couple of days had passed without us talking – this was not something we'd ever done before. It seemed like I had a lot of interesting news, but none of it would be easy to explain over text message, and possibly he knew about some of it anyway, given that Chris L was his impending housemate.

What did boys talk about, other than grief and longing? Clothes, I thought senselessly. Boys talk about clothes.

'Dan,' I texted. 'I'm in Richmond. My clothes are very gross.' This was true, but irrelevant. I'd moved on from my own clothes, which were in the washing basket; I wore Vivian's clean clothes, which were oversized but comfy, silhouettes that had passed over Chris L and now to me.

When there wasn't an instant reply, I wrote, 'Could you bring me my clothes?'

A few hours passed before he wrote to me.

'Hey there,' he wrote, 'to be honest with you, I am not having the best week, unforch. I think some time apart right now is good for us, unforch. It's hard for me to contemplate moving in with Lachlan and the more I talk to you the harder it will be.'

There followed some logistical proposals.

He'd paid his rent for most of January, it had come

out before Christmas, before he and Lachlan had decided in a coke-edged fervour that now was the time to accelerate their domestic dreams, even if it meant sharing the apartment with Chris L.

Four weeks was a normal, even generous, amount of notice, and while it still did not solve the basic problem that I didn't want him to leave, it gave me plenty of time to think about my options.

He asked if I minded him going into my room and packing his missing wine glasses, which I found alarming: either he was already at a very late stage of packing, ready to action his fragile top-of-the-box things, or he was going to move out in a piecemeal fashion, which would be difficult to argue with but all the more painful for me.

I was also injured by his double-unforching, the careless use of an abbreviation that was cute exactly once. It would've been so easy for him to glance back up the message and make sure it looked careful, composed and clean.

On the other hand, there was the message itself – lush, composed and clean. The age of dad-texting seemed to be over.

'Very cool bro,' I wrote back to him. 'Very cool and good.'

I thought the phone was vibrating, but it was just my shaking hand.

It was dusk now, the mosquito hour, and Vivian was out. The past couple of days had shown me that he could be out at any time, always returning with avocados and bread. I knew from tell-tale Grindr sounds, those soft, quick, crunchy bloops, that he was probably ducking out and hooking up with other people, and why shouldn't he, it was his vacation, his summer in Melbourne. It was obvious that I'd never been able to find him on Grindr because he'd blocked me, presumably on the first afternoon I'd visited him. I respected this. It mitigated my actual sadness, about Dan, with a veil of something else, something sad but irrelevant, even soapy.

I stared out the window, drank another cupboard beer, went flicking through the Lonely Planet guides to Melbourne. If I stayed at Vivian's much longer, I would have to sign up to the Yarra Libraries or find work.

Then a message on my phone.

'Do you need something to think about?'

Dan.

'One vegetable. All five vowels. No online searching. Go.'

I thought about it. This was horrible. Aubergine? No *o*.

'All five vowels in order?' I asked.

'What do you think?' he wrote.

I stared at the phone. 'No,' I wrote.

'That's right,' he wrote. 'No. Happy holidays "bro" ☺.'

Happy holidays indeed. I was stuck here. I knew I could always go home and get the clothes myself, but the idea of Dan packing was enough to stop me.

You always heard that life was in the business of closing doors, that character was formed through people doing what they had to, having the courage to square up to things unknown – whooshing, very dangerous, and nonetheless they jumped. But all I'd found this summer was that when one door closed, another opened; it was all entrance and egress, and never the last one, a dumb series of ouroborosing substitutes.

After a few nights, the inevitable happened. I got sick of sleeping on the couch. The silk sheets started to look good. I wanted a better space; I wanted the bed. And lacking the traditional, military means of land acquisition, I knew that I would have to resort to private resources.

I would 'go to him'.

I waited till long after midnight, in case he'd had sex with someone when he'd gone out at lunch. I stepped to the side of the bed, watched Vivian quietly respiring. In the end, I climbed in with him because

I was paranoid that he knew I was there anyway, knew I was watching, and to watch and leave would have been creepier again.

'Vivian,' I whispered.

'Mmmmmmm,' he said.

He threw his arm over my side and went back to sleep, his face breathing pleasantly not quite against my neck. After a long time, I relaxed and I went to sleep as well – and this was exactly how we continued.

This was too much. Not a nightmare, but a dream! It got very upsetting knowing he would leave the country at an unspecified hour, presumably soon. Part of me started to think I'd stay with him forever. Vivian, his mind closed up, like a sealed banana, but with less need for small talk and a stronger property portfolio. In other words, this was almost an age of perfect peace – and long after these men in my life had become the boys of my youth, I would remember this apartment, small, breezy and private, as the first time I experienced this special way of life, one where people coexisted in amiable silence.

I preferred a creaky environment, of violent achievements. But I liked knowing I had a self when not composed of listening and talking through walls and drinking wine all day. What's more, it seemed clear that I would always be okay in uncertainty and occasional flashes of its opposite, that change wasn't really a referendum on the self, just as a specific shift in cloudiness or temperature didn't invalidate the experience of weather. This finding may have lacked ballast. But I had never tested it. Companionate love, the internet told me, was a necessary evil, a path towards which many people unwillingly stumble, but here I was, achieving it in just a few days. Early in the mornings, I woke up before Vivian. When cars outside were rushing back and forth, north and south and back again, I could almost forget that he was breathing.

Of course this couldn't last, and of course it didn't. The fourth or fifth night, not even mid-January, we were gearing up for another round of avo on toast, but this time I demanded variation. Vivian went out and came home with a jar of Vegemite. I approved and watched him fixing me the meal. My eyes went wide. 'Whoa,' I said. He spread an exorbitant quantity, like it was peanut butter or jam. He smiled at me. He spread some more. I watched in fascination.

He raised the toast to his mouth and took a bite.

His mouth twisted.

I had been so wrong. A failure of attention, the cost of my comforts. Vivian was American. Not an

Australian in New York. American. I felt like a weird other shoe had dropped.

I had operated under a series of self-inflicted misunderstandings. He was renting this apartment. He had rented the beach house. 'My gift,' he smiled, 'to each of you. For showing me around all month and hanging out with me. Who are you texting?'

I was texting Dan. 'Dan, get me out of here,' I wrote.

Vivian looked edgy.

'Now are you leaving me?' he said.

Vibrations in my pocket.

'I have to look at this,' I said.

The message read: 'I can come over at 8pm if that suits.'

I was so happy with Dan right then. He understood the urgency.

But I was shocked by the new formality. Was this now who we were?

I had always wanted a friend who was willing to do what suits.

I clutched Dan when he got there. He wore brown boots, red socks, green stretchy shorts, and a baggy, tucked-in shirt in dreamy powder-blue.

'Dan,' I breathed. 'This is a sartorial metamorphosis. How long have you been planning this?'

'It's my late summer look.'

I pulled back. 'It's barely January. Late summer my foot.'

'I go back to work tomorrow,' he shrugged. 'The year has begun.'

'You look amazingly awesome,' I said.

'Are you sleeping here?'

I nodded.

'Cool. Where?'

I gestured into the bedroom. Vivian had gone out again, to do whatever he was doing.

We sat on the couch. I told Dan about Vivian's convalescence. He leaned in, sniffed the couch blanket, which had gone unwashed, and said, 'The fluid you smelled was literally just sweat. This is why I was right to make you go out and meet people. Everyone should be able to interpret human scents.'

I remained sceptical; it had been a lot of sweat. And I know this is a normal feature of colds and feverish flus, but I could not shake – and still can't shake – the sense that Vivian had returned from somewhere mineral, as someone elemental. I knew this would be very unconvincing if said out loud.

'Dan,' I said, 'where are my clothes?'

'I didn't bring any,' he said. 'Because I'm taking you home. What are you even doing here? Where are we? What is this place?'

'You know that we're in Richmond,' I said. 'You're not taking me home.'

'Clearly,' he said, and my heart was full. When I die, while other people's lives are flashing before their eyes, I will just see Dan perched on the arm of a couch and saying the word 'clearly' in an unimpressed tone. And I know, I wanted to tell him, that you can't take me home, because it will not be the place that I mean by that word.

He walked through the apartment, just *looking* at everything. When he was done inspecting, he said, 'Do you know what? I worry.'

'Don't pretend you're worried,' I said. 'You aren't worrying. You're judging.'

He held out his hands. 'I'm not judging!'

'He sleeps on silk,' I complained.

He wrinkled up his nose, but then said, 'That's okay! He didn't pick it.'

'You knew he was American?'

He looked at me strangely. 'What do you mean? Everyone does.'

I shook my head; it was too dumb, a horror of inattention. I still didn't understand the implications of my mistake.

'Be proud of me, Dan,' I told him. 'I'm doing excellent things.' I explained it, or the non of it. How my days here at Vivian's had beautifully confirmed that love as a raw, full phenomenon was really not for me, that I preferred this other business, polite and distant. 'I'm facing up to the unknown but chosen.' I grinned.

'Ugh,' he said. 'I hate that phrase. Where did it even come from?'

'It came from a guy who drinks in the morning.'

'Oh yeah, that guy,' he said. 'I've been thinking about him. Why's it so amazing to jump into the unknown? God forbid a universe in which people make considered and informed decisions about their own lives. Except right now,' he added. 'I want you to do as I say.'

He held out his fist, and opened it. Inside were Lachlan's car keys.

'Come for a drive with me. I miss you,' he said.

'Do you promise you aren't just driving me home? Because that would be kidnapping.'

'I swear.'

We both understood this might mean nothing.

We got into Lachlan's car, me in the passenger seat, and Dan drove the two of us through the hilly Richmond streets, lined with trees and swooping into bowl-shaped cul-de-sacs. We did not spot Vivian, the Richmond Man, or anyone.

'Where are we going?' I said.

'Nowhere,' he said.

'This is new,' I said.

'Yes, I have been profoundly changed by the availability of Lachlan's car,' he said.

'Really,' I said. 'In what way?'

'The main thing,' he said, 'is that I sometimes drive his car.'

We moved into a new suburb, full of lovely houses. I couldn't believe how wonderful the houses were; like the lovely deco outsides of Vivian's apartment, but detached, pastel, single-storey, double-storey. With turrets.

'Guess which suburb we're in,' he said.

'St Kilda,' I said.

'Your sense of direction is terrible.'

'Eltham,' I breathed.

'Elwood,' he corrected.

'Elllll-woood,' I said. 'Interesting. Why don't we have nice houses like these on the north-side?'

'It's because we're better people,' he said, 'and can bear more hardship.'

I was getting sad. It was proximity to Dan, and proximity to the future he was building for himself; out here, in a house, with a mortgage, with his plants; with monogamy, with a marriage, with a baby, in a pram. Why were all these things so incompatible with my values? And what good were my values if I'd only stolen what had been Dan's, which he had stolen anyway from other, better people, people who were not young and male and cis and white? Didn't he know I was prepared to agree with him, on anything? I would have followed Dan anywhere, with sufficient warning, yes to selling out but also just to hell. I was blindsided. Why hadn't he warned me?

He yanked the car to the kerb so hard I was neck-shocked and then we both sat there with the motor running. Above us, trees not moving, around us, no one walking, just letterboxes and flowerpots in this beautiful dark street.

'What. Happened. To. My. Shoes,' he said.

I sang like a canary: the hot tub adventure, and taking his shoes, and making out on the beach with Vivian, and the sudden progress into bloody denouement. I paused before describing Vivian's HIV freak-out; it was too lame and too douchey, but I told him anyway.

'I don't know. He's super old. He doesn't know what it means. Anyway,' I said, 'I gave him a pretty good scare.'

Dan nodded. He put the car in reverse and pulled out of the parking space, drove for half a minute, then dramatically twisted the car into another park.

He stared straight through the windshield, and not at me, not once.

'Did you know,' he said, 'that if I playfully lied about my serostatus, I could playfully go to jail?'

I did not know how to respond to this – of course I knew, of course.

'Well,' he said to my silence, 'you had your own personal AIDS crisis. Was it very significant?'

'Yes.'

'Cathartic?'

'Yes.'

'And are you finished?' he said.

I paused. 'Yes.'

'Good,' he said.

'I'm so sad that you're leaving,' I said.

'I know you are. You cried!'

'You don't know that,' I seethed. He definitely did. 'You really don't think things went wrong?'

'Nope. Everything went right.'

'That's nice of you,' I said. 'I don't want to live with anyone else.'

'I know you don't,' he said.

'You're going to get married,' I said.

'Stop it,' he said. 'I'm still really, really, really mad about the shoes.' He drummed his fingers on the dashboard.

'How can I make it up to you?'

He glared at me.

'I don't really . . . work,' I said.

'I just feel so *bad*,' he said. 'All I want to do is settle down with Lachlan and touch his arms and think about interior design.'

'That's okay, Dan,' I said.

'I dream about those towels!'

'You steal them from entrepreneurs. So that is still quite rebellious.'

'Not really,' he said, his head in his hands. 'I think it's overstock.'

We both stared out the window. Nothing could have been bleaker. Somehow we'd wound up talking about consumer goods. I felt like *this* was the towel game, the persistence of things that had not previously mattered to us but now irrevocably did. It was horrible how so much of life recently had turned on drinking and talking, driving and phones. If you spent enough time doing anything, anything could curdle. When you put it like that, obviously he was moving out.

He cranked the ignition.

'Let's go,' he said.

'Yeah, see ya Eltham.'

We drove back to Richmond. I felt high and tired and free. But when Dan parked outside Vivian's, his face was cool and grim.

'What are you going to do,' he asked me, 'without my protection?'

My heart sank. But there you go, we were getting down to business. I *had* been under his protection. We'd just never said so.

'I think I have to stay here for now,' I said.

'I agree,' he said. 'Do you really like Vivian?'

I thought about it. 'I don't know,' I said.

'As a boyfriend, or a person?'

I liked the way he phrased that, like they couldn't be the same thing.

'I don't know,' I said again. 'Can the answer be neither?'

He frowned. 'I'm not sure I should say this?'

'No, go.'

'How old is Vivian?'

I didn't know. For many reasons, I should have checked his passport. 'Let's say thirty-one.'

'Picture yourself at thirty-one.'

I closed my eyes.

'What do you see?'

I saw . . . a blank space.

'I don't want to tell you,' I said.

'That's okay,' he said. 'My point is, do you really see yourself looking back over your twenties and saying, Yeah, I guess sex just never really took off for me?'

I hadn't looked at it this way, and I didn't see his point. I knew I would someday, potentially someday soon, find someone I wanted to screw, who also wanted to screw me, and would happen to do so at the appropriate moment, turning me into a sex person – a converting agent indeed. Maybe there'd be many someones, like when an old croc gets its first taste of human flesh and now it's a shootable maneater. But just as much, I understood that this might *never* happen. I would stay the same, and only the perception would be different; I'd be frigid in one decade, choosy in the next.

But I had to concede that none of these possibilities produced the feeling that, someday, I might find myself in a warm location, desperate to make a mopey person lie in bed with me, someone I didn't really seem to be attracted to, or have anything in common with. I remembered the sneer.

'He can't get enough of my personality,' I blurted. 'I'm irresistible to Vivian.'

Dan stared at me. 'You know what, I think this will end well for you. You'll be okay eventually.'

'Okay and unclothed,' I said.

'Clearly, I brought you clothes,' he said. 'Feel free to grab them from the boot when you go.'

'Dan,' I said. 'You've really surprised me.'

He popped the boot. 'You know what they say about assumptions,' he said.

'What?'

He jabbed the air with his finger.

'Don't make 'em!'

I went upstairs exhilarated. Had that really happened? Really, it was a reminder of how bad things had been, even if Dan wanted to convince me otherwise. We used to have nights talking like that, in autumn and winter. What if now that he was leaving, our relationship could be . . . good?

Still, it left me uneasy – as if a vacuum pack had sealed itself around me here in Richmond, and now it had been pierced and summer air was rushing in. What *did* I offer Vivian? It wasn't like I made him food or paid his bills or cleaned. It wasn't like I was particularly easy to be around, either.

When I got upstairs Vivian was in bed already, the lights off, the sheet on him. I stripped off most of my clothes and crawled into the bed, and pulled both of his arms around my stomach.

'How was Dan?' he whispered.

'Good,' I said.

I pulled his arms more tightly in. There was silence and darkness. Then:

'When are you going to propose?' he said.

It all fell down like summer rain, the answer, the secret motive. When had he turned from skeezily, breezily half-available to suddenly and drastically voracious for me? When Chris L had revealed that he was married to a person, somebody who maybe lived in Sydney. I had not been lovable; I had been available. Like many a fiancé, I had been a dupe.

What I really wanted was to make myself throw up. 'Excuse me,' I said. I went to the bathroom and attempted it.

But try as I might, I couldn't summon the necessary ire. For one thing, I sort of admired Vivian's perfect sneakiness, which may have been one of my more compromised admirations. It was perfect because it didn't require much sneakiness at all, just selecting a subject who was practically poised to do the work for you. For another thing, it gave me a sting of pleasure to have been tricked in this classical way. Since the plebiscite, since the yes vote, I, too, could be married for my visa-granting capacity, tricked by a stranger who saw that I was lonely. I felt very free, strangely accepted. The truest gifts were complicated indeed.

All bets were off now. I could do as I liked. And this too was awful – to do as one liked was to invite experience, culmination, victors, losers – but it was my great luck to be struck here by the obvious: that the alternative, to stay in the apartment, was worse.

In the morning, I bundled up my things and stepped into the sunlight, hot and early, before Vivian was up.

That was what I wanted, to move out and not look back. I harboured no ill feelings for this person who had only had his eyes on citizenship and made use of a resource to get it, even if the resource had happened to be me. I didn't want to be the one who left or the one who lost, but even so, as if this were the only choice, I left.

I was outside in my own clothes, with a plastic bag of belongings, a charged phone in my other hand, mapping out the route – I would take the 109 all the way to Elizabeth Street and then I would take the 19 north to Barkly Square – when I looked up to the window of the stranger's apartment, and finally I saw somebody gazing down at me.

I bit my lip and breathed in and began to wave my hand – and, just then, another figure emerged from behind the stranger, wrapped their arms around him, and encircled him close and tight.

'That's so weird,' a voice said. 'There's someone in my apartment.'

I turned around and there he was: my friend, the Richmond Man, holding a gym bag and his car keys, looking fresh.

'No,' he said, 'I don't think there's anyone in my apartment. I hope not, anyway. That's someone else's window.'

I smiled. He was super dorky, warm, safe and familiar. I knew this genre: home-invasion humour.

'Why are you here?' he asked me.

In a certain light, what question is not existential?

'Why are *you* here?' I asked.

'Good question,' he said. 'And simple to answer. I'm just about to drive to Brunswick to go to the gym. I asked you first. You still have to answer me.'

But I was saved from this problem by the arrival of the ending, which came to me like another gift, foolish and unbidden. I walked up to my Richmond friend and kissed him on the mouth. He kissed me back. It was neutral and lovely; that's how a mouth could taste, as long as you were busy thinking about real estate.

'How much rent do you pay?'

He told me.

'That's ridiculous,' I said. 'Why don't you move to Brunswick?'

'Hmm. I don't know,' he said.

'Even more reason,' I enthused. 'This is the unknown but chosen. Maybe we'll live well together. Don't you want to know?'

Goodbye, Richmond, I thought again, climbing into his car – the suburb where my fate had split on two sides of a road, and everything was failure, whichever side I chose. I'd behaved inconsistently in the stony name of justice, and behaved ineffectively in the human name of love, and instead of making all the difference, it had all made none. I was catching a ride in the opposite direction.

'The unknown but chosen,' he said. 'I like that idea.'

He looked at me and looked away again.

Classic him.

Classic me.

A few days after the stranger drove me back to Brunswick, he agreed to my offer and was planning to move in.

'And what did you do in *this* room?' the stranger was saying.

'I slept in the bed and looked at my phone and read my books,' I said.

'Wow. And what did you do in *this* room?'

'This was Dan's room. He looked at his laptop.'

'Wow.'

Although I had his number, I still hadn't managed to discover his name, not because I didn't care, but because I cared too much; it was simply too late in our friendship to ask, because I would look literally insane for inviting him to live with me without first knowing this, his most basic detail. Although this made it very funny to discuss with Dan, I was looking forward to the day he signed the tenant transfer form and I could put an end to yet another puzzle.

'And what about *this* room?' he was saying.

He was testing my patience.

'This room is the hallway,' I said. 'We just have to walk through it.'

'And what did you do in *this* room?'

We'd now come to the kitchen. It had been a reading space, not a conversation space. Now it was a space of many questions, or not even that: there was just this simple question, repeated ad nauseam. 'We ate in the kitchen,' I snapped. 'That's all we did in here.'

We smiled at each other.

'I'm running out of locations,' I said. 'That's kind of the whole thing.'

He looked at me meaningfully. 'Thank you for the house tour,' he said, and took a step and hugged me. I stood there limply for a minute, but remembered that the thing with change was to embrace it, like he was embracing me. I patted his back. I gritted my teeth and squished his ribs.

'Such a nice person,' I enthused to Dan.

'Oh please,' he said. 'Because he thanked you for the house tour? I thank you for everything.'

'I'd thank you to list them.'

'I don't keep records of my thank yous,' he said. 'But you know what, you should. You don't say thank you to anyone, and you don't say sorry either.'

'That's not true,' I said.

Lachlan sucked in his breath.

'No, Lachlan, don't breathe like that,' I said. If Lachlan noticed this behaviour, and verified it, it was probably real. Did I really not say sorry or thank you? Not to Dan, not to Lachlan, not to my friend from Richmond, not to Chris L, not to Vivian, not to anyone? I was *sure* I had said one of those things, to someone, at some point. Everyone has, they are almost grammar.

But I was creeped out about this possibility of rudeness, that I didn't say thank you or sorry in the spirit that was expected. I had always thought I was nicer than Dan – he was abrupt and strident. But maybe he could get away with abruptness and stridence because he couched it correctly, because he picked the right times, times when it was desired, even needed?

'Anyway,' I told them, 'the substance of the tour was about all the things we did together and how much I liked them. You should be pleased.'

'I'm sorry,' he said.

'Thanks,' I said.

'How did that feel?' he said.

'Normal,' I said. 'It's a normal word that I use all the time.'

I adjusted my sunglasses. I tugged nervously at my scarf.

I was meeting Dan and Lachlan at a café on Napier Street, where we had nabbed a couple of its prized outdoor chairs.

'I wish you'd take the scarf off,' said Dan. 'It's obviously too hot.'

I touched the scarf. 'It is my tender tribute,' I said.

I could not afford nice shawls like Chris L, or I did not have the taste, so I had gone to Savers on Sydney Road on Friday and asked a roving person where I could find the *shawls*, whispering like I was at a sex shop. She smiled at me. 'Actually it's complicated,' she said. 'They're clothes, but because they're shawls, we hang them with the sheets.' Complications into clothes, shawls into sheets: even at Savers the world had a frictionless quality, like anything could be swapped out of existence, even me.

I had shown up at the café wrapped in this heavy scarf, this thick brown one I had seized in a fit of dark unreason, because I could not find a light shawl and I did not want a sheet and it turned out the large scarves were hung there also. Another thing that Savers had was giant bug-eyed sunglasses, plenty of them, heaps of them, perfect for accessory-ruiners. I had bought a handful of them and wore a pair with pride.

'You don't think the scarf's *appropriate*?' I said.

'I don't know what to say,' said Dan. 'It's very low-hanging fruit.'

'What has Chris L been wearing lately?'

He leaned back and crossed his arms.

'Don't be maudlin,' he said.

'I'm not being maudlin,' I said. 'I'm asking a question.'

'You're putting us all in an uncomfortable position,' said Dan. 'He has housemate privileges. You're my friend.'

My body had come out of my body, and crawled across the floor, and into another apartment where Chris L happened to live, sharing a wall with Dan just the way that I had.

'Would it be *so* terrible if you gave me *one* fashion tip from Chris L?' His Instagram had been no help, ever. It had always been a veil, a young man in a silver cape in good light, in bad. I clung to the crumbs of him, like they'd turn into bread.

'It wouldn't be so terrible,' Dan said. 'I don't think he'd care. But I think it would be good for you to accept he's gone.'

'That's not fair.'

'It's really fair.'

Lachlan tipped his head and frowned, fairness-agreeing, like my fortune had been levered out of a fairness machine.

'Are you okay?' asked Dan.

I stared at him.

'*Cauliflower*,' I said.

'Yes!' he said. 'One vegetable, all five vowels. Yes,' he clapped.

Life was in the business of closing doors, it's true; as for which doors, if I didn't want to tempt the wrath of hell, maybe it was best not to be picky.

It was in the spirit of giving up, which was a kind of hobby, that I left the scarf behind me and went with Dan and Lachlan to our planned Saturday activity, which was going to the gym above the Fitzroy Pool. Dan had convinced me it was not that far from home – it wasn't, just a mid-length walk, then the 96, then more walking – and also a nice way that we could hang out and be friends, and, what a dog I was, of course I had said yes. I also planned to buy a bike roughly as soon as possible, once I had got my summer job, or autumn job, whatever. I had come to like the sound of many of these changes, but it seemed unwise to say so, almost an admission. Something told me I should keep my defeat close to my chest, that to let it go prematurely was a material risk. It seemed right for this to be a time of wound-licking.

But the pool reached out with its fat claw and pulled me in with its fit hand. We got changed in the changing rooms and then walked up to the gym. We went through all of the annoying motions.

The temperature was thirty-six degrees, and the industrial fans were helpless. If I hadn't previously known what real sweat smelled like I did now, alternately stale and very pungent.

Finally we were done, and Lachlan, like a flash, was in his swimmers, towel in hand, this time a sensible beach towel, out the doors and scaling the ever-crowded bleachers.

'Coming?' said Dan.

'I reallllly can't go out there,' I said. 'It's just way too social and I hate it and I'm scared.'

'Nobody else thinks that! I promise you,' he said.

'Dan,' I said, 'don't gaslight me. You're part of the problem.'

'It's not a problem,' he said, 'it's a pool.'

I looked out the glass doors that separated gym from pool and tried to see the bleachers the way he apparently did. It was just a pool. There were a lot of boys out there, there really was a lot of sweat and not a lot of room.

'I don't know Dan,' I said. 'I just don't really want to.'

'You're gaslighting yourself,' he said. 'Keep looking.'

I looked outside. I looked and looked. I looked and I kept looking. And mayyybe I could see the thing he wanted me to see. Yes, among the cruisy boys were lots of kinds of people, people I didn't see when I let my eyes unfocus until I saw a few of them to the exclusion of all else. But this wasn't the only point, that I had looked at them because I knew I could learn from them, or because they were a bit like Dan, internet and sex people who'd upgraded into friends. It was that I hadn't seen even *these* people, not completely. It was Speedos all the way down, the whole world, the whole thing.

I had a sudden and unshakeable faith in this idea, always a sign that things are going well and you should be cleared for take-off.

'Right,' I said uneasily. Was this what Dan meant? Maybe I could go out there. Something was holding me back.

It was Dan's hand, and it had cupped my shoulder. 'Please come outside,' he said.

I looked at him softly.

'I'm sorry,' I said, 'I'm just not risking it.'

'You have to do something,' he said. 'Go to the steam room.'

I said, 'Really?' I looked up at the sun. 'Even in summer?'

'You'll like it.' He rolled his eyes. 'It'll be empty.'

And it was steamy, and empty, a lovely salty place – a world within a universe, its superheated middle. I breathed in through my nostrils and out through my mouth and watched the droplets form in gluey grids along the ceiling. It was thirty-six degrees outside and objectively unpleasant, but Dan was right. That really was the part I liked the best.

I breathed in steam and breathed steam out, a steamy wet environment. You couldn't live in a steam room, but you could always visit.

In the weeks between my leaving Richmond and Dan leaving for good, the main thing I did was walk around endlessly, avoiding the various boxes Dan had left un-taped, half-packed.

I walked Nicholson Street, Johnston Street, Smith Street, random others. I could have gone to West Brunswick, or south into the city, but instead I walked all the boring streets I knew already, hoping that the man in the shawl, the news that walked like a man, would walk like news or person into a run-in with me.

In other words, I was stalking Chris L. But not, like, stalking-stalking. A few times I'd deliberately passed Dan and Lachlan's warehouse apartment building when I knew neither of them were in and was tempted to press the buzzer so I could say my piece. But I knew I wouldn't personally like being surprised like this, and if I was halfway right in my Chris L theory-of-mind – that we were both private people who expressed it differently – I knew that this could only wreck things further.

So, like a creep, I staked out the apartment, hanging out at a bar where I could see the mouth of the street. I was wearing my sunglasses but they were no protection; they didn't hide the shape of the person, only their intentions.

Just as I was giving up, my pint gone flat and warm, I saw the old, mysterious shape exit the apartment, an alluring stranger in a storm of teal. My instinct was to duck, but my action was to freeze. He passed me without looking, holding a green bag.

I tailed him at a safe distance into the Smith Street Coles, where Dan had either gone or not gone in quest of sherry vinegar. But I couldn't find him when I snuck in.

I wandered down the health food aisle, and down the aisle of snacks, and down the aisle of rice and soups, and through the stacks of fruits.

There were all kinds of people here but none of them was him.

When I looked at my phone, the message had come in ten minutes prior: 'Don't follow me,' it said.

'Chris L,' I wrote, 'I just want to talk to you.'

No reply. I wandered home, defeated.

Later that night, the reply came: 'Why?' he wrote.

I didn't know what to say. What was I doing? It was ridiculous.

'Because I live with Dan?' he wrote. 'So we should all be friends?'

When he put it like that, it sounded pretty specious. And it wasn't even the real reason; I wanted to be friends with him, not him-among-the-many. This I could admit to myself, definitely not to him.

'Don't worry about it,' I texted.

'Is there anything else?' he wrote.

I let the screen go black.

Dan finally came by to clean the gross dregs of his bedroom and pick up the last of his things at the latest possible moment, the night before my Richmond friend was scheduled to move in. He managed to bequeath me all his least-appealing plants.

'You don't want them,' he said happily.

'I really don't,' I agreed. 'Thank you, Dan.'

'You won't kill them, will you?'

'We'll all find out together,' I said.

He crouched to wipe a skirting board and then looked up at me. 'Hey, you said thank you.'

'Ohhh, did I?' I said.

I tried to play it cool, but the truth was that I'd taken his critique to heart, about thank you and sorry, because if we cannot be civil, then what can we be? It had been a conscious effort, and the words felt strange to speak, like an unfamiliar tongue touching the old familiar cavity. Thank you, I had started mouthing crazily. Sorry.

I wandered back into my room without even thinking and only when I'd been looking at my phone for a while did I realise I was wasting our last night on the planet, which had felt so normal for a minute, despite the diminishing debris, that it had also seemed consummately wastable. I started doing my automatic hair-smoothing again and was just trying to suppress this when Dan appeared in the doorway and deus-ex-machinaed me. 'Come look at the skirting boards,' he said.

I followed him into the bedroom. 'Very beautiful,' I said, although they were not beautiful, they were still skirting boards, just clean.

'Well,' he said, dusting his hands of dust, of house, of me. 'There's nothing left to say to each other. It was fun living with you.'

'Shh,' I said. It was not always fun. 'Should we get food?'

'Sure.'

'Uber Eats?'

'No!' He took out his phone and pretended to be a grumpy person waiting for their meal, staring at the phone and shaking the screen. 'Why are you going *that* way? No, why are you going *that* way?' He shook it again. 'They're real people, they're not pneumatic tubes. What do you have in the kitchen?'

'I . . . don't want to tell you,' I said.

In the rusting refrigerator, which he would leave with me, was an open jar of gherkins, a tub of Nuttelex, and a plastic bag of trusty bread.

'Why are you keeping the bread in the fridge? You are a whole new person.'

I had done this because otherwise it looked too serial-killerish, gherkins and Nuttelex in the fridge and nothing else. I tried putting a bag of rice in there but somehow it looked worse.

I explained this. 'It still looks pretty serial-killerish,' he said.

'Nooo,' I said, inspecting it. 'Good things come in threes. Do you want a gherkin sandwich?'

'I guess so,' he said.

We sat up on the sloping balcony, munching on our sandwiches, watching distant joggers jog through Princes Park.

'I should've used the park more,' he said.

'You should've done a lot of things.'

He looked at me. 'Like what?' he said.

'I don't know,' I sighed. 'Probably nothing. You should have no regrets about your time in Brunswick.'

He swallowed the last part of his sandwich.

'You don't have to live with this person,' he said. 'I wish you wouldn't do that. It's concerning that he's literally the first person you asked.'

'Not even really asked,' I said.

'Not even really person.'

'Where is he right now?' I sighed. I looked at the park speculatively. But I knew he was probably home in Richmond, packing. Although it would be nice if every answer was revealing, sometimes they only revealed the dimness of the question. And then the stupid questioners had their own complications, bringing in their foolish minds and bitter histories.

'I don't really have a choice,' I said. 'I'm not going to leave Brunswick.'

'I know you aren't,' he said.

'He is the best available option.'

What would me and Dan be now, without the shared address? He wasn't like a normal friend. He was something different. Would I even have this friendship without the symptoms of it? If it was undetectable, what even was it? The only thing we live with is the spectacle of hours, the certainty that everything can not be what it seems – not space, not air, not blood, not skin, not friendship, and not difference – but what it seems? That's the only thing it isn't.

He put his arms around me, encircling without touching, and then he stood up and then he left.

I breathed.

'Wait,' Dan said.

He re-emerged onto the balcony.

'I do have one regret, actually. Do you trust me?'

I rolled my eyes. 'Of course I do,' I said.

'Then give me your phone.'

I frowned at Dan.

'No, give me your phone,' he said.

I did so.

'Unlock it.'

I took it, entered my PIN, and handed the phone back to him.

'Give me a second.' He seemed very excited, even giddy, and I'd learned to be afraid of him in this impassioned state. He could be wicked, very punishing – dealing out justice, a selfish angel, solving only problems that happened to impact him.

'Do I have to leave the balcony?' I said.

'No, that's okay,' he said, and stepped inside and huddled over the phone, concealing his actions.

'I'm finished,' he said.

I stepped inside.

He gave the phone back.

'What did you do?' I asked him.

'I'm not telling,' he said.

I went to say something else but he raised his hand to stop me.

'Please don't ruin this. Love you,' he said.

He ran down the stairs, leaving those mad syllables hanging.

The longest night! I quaked and moaned. What would daylight bring me – the unseen hand, the lick of fate, the natural conclusion?

I pored through my phone, of course, but Dan had erased his workings; if he'd sent a text message, he'd covered his tracks; if he'd deleted a phone number, I didn't miss it. I paid special attention to the Richmond Man's text thread, because what if my best and ugliest fantasy was real: that he'd vanquished the stranger, told him not to move in, because he'd discovered Brunswick was 'not finished with him yet' – whether that meant something terrible or lovely.

So Dan came back to Brunswick . . . he and Lachlan were cool . . . they were happiest with distance . . . my presence was key. There was no end to my fantasies. I knew they were unsupportable.

In the morning, I made my coffee and sat at

the table, preparing myself for disappointment and triumph.

The Richmond Man was due today, but hours later – nothing. I called him. He did not pick up. He did not respond to messages. Maybe he was busy lifting boxes . . .

I paced around the kitchen, made more coffee. I texted Dan. 'What's going on?' Nothing.

But just as I'd come to believe that nothing else would happen, the most horrible sound: a heavy vehicle, beeping and stopping, backing slowly into a space on the street outside the house. The moving van was here – and with it, my future.

And then the message hit my phone:

'I accept your apology.'

I stared at this. I glanced up the screen, but the last message was from *him* and it said 'Is there anything else?' – a question he'd sent after he'd dodged me on Smith Street, a question I'd not been prepared to answer at that time.

A knock at the door. I looked at it.

I knew what was out there. And how neat was this solution – two inconvenient housemates, and Dan had managed to get rid of both of us at once.

'Ugh,' I texted Dan.

But the truth is I wasn't mad, I was frightened. By the mettle this would take – its ordinariness, its substance. The things this friend would ask of me were of a different order. There would be steep requirements. I wasn't up to the job. And still the knocks kept coming.

I walked to the door and opened it, the big moment was here. I saw the silver fabric, which was held up like a screen, bouncing back the ripest sun of January. And it had brought its things with it, a truck of new mysteries, hauled here from an apartment that I had never seen.

'Should I come in?' he asked me.

I had no idea.

Goodbye, Dan, and thank you for the complicated gift.

ACKNOWLEDGEMENTS

In devising a story that covers eight weeks from a limited perspective, I did so in conversation with a number of histories and lived realities that are only briefly indicated in the book, some quite obliquely. While this novel was written with faith in the unsaid, here I recognise the existence of the unsaid and would like to indicate my respect for it.

This novel would be nowhere without Marya Spence, so thank you, Marya, and thank you, Clare Mao, for working very hard on its behalf. Thank you, Cullen Stanley for representing it in Australia, Cate Blake for acquiring it and breaking down its structure, Johannes Jakob for an exacting and even-handed edit, and Nikki Christer for publishing it with imagination and judgement. Thanks to Bella Arnott-Hoare for publicising it well, and to Laura Thomas for designing a perfect cover.

To colleagues who offered edits, interviews, and other professional services on various versions of the manuscript: Anna Barnes, Emily Bitto, Amy Bloom, Sam Cooney, Marieke Hardy, Nic Holas, Patrick Kelly, Krissy Kneen, Ben Law, Peter Polites, Paul Dalla Rosa, Josephine Rowe, Ellena Savage, Chris Somerville, Sofija Stefanovic, Estelle Tang, Shane Tas, Anna Thwaites, Christos Tsiolkas, Sam Twyford-Moore, Sam Wallman, Bryan Washington, Fiona Wright and Lorelei Vashti – thank you! I'm especially grateful to an anonymous interviewee and reader who improved the work considerably at two decisive moments, as did Dion Kagan, by letting me read an early copy of his wonderful book *Positive Images: Gay Men and HIV/AIDS in the Culture of 'Post-Crisis'* (I.B. Tauris, 2018). The following organisations were critical providers of money, time and validation: the Australia Council for the Arts, the City of Melbourne Annual Arts Grants, the Felix Meyer Scholarship, non/fictionLab's McCraith House and the MacDowell Colony. Extra strength, triple platinum, high quality support was courtesy of Nikki Lusk, Michaela McGuire, Tim McGuire, Ruby Murray and Liam Pieper.

ACKNOWLEDGEMENTS

A giant thanks to RMIT, especially the flipped PRS group, the novelLab and non/fictionLab research groups and everyone in the Writing and Publishing discipline: it's an excellent place for writers and a true professional home.

To my extremely supportive family – I dedicate the book to you.

My friends have far and away been the biggest part of my life in the time the book was written; in addition to the above, thank you, Al, Taube, Shannon, Marty, Pete, Ben, Miles, Ferdy, Katie, James, Kristy, Nisha, Luke, Adam, Bec, Tristan, Bec, Tristan, Michael, Claire, JB, Matt, Marion, Shaun, Jeremy, Britt, Kate, Steph, Toby, Kate, Matt, Jake, Alice, John, Jimmy, Brooke, Daina, Tahnee, Rob, Liz, Virginia, Ellen and both of the book clubs.

A final thanks to Jarrod Sturnieks, who's been there from the start. 'Totally essential to the creation of this work' doesn't even begin to cover it.

Most of this story was written on stolen land.